CONVERSION OF A PIMP: JOSEPH

Copyright © 2015 by Angela Moore

All rights reserved. This book or any portion thereof may not be reproduced stored in or introduced into a retrieval system, or transmitted in any manner (electronic, mechanical, photocopying, recording or otherwise) whatsoever without the express written permission of the copyright owner except by a reviewer who may quote brief passages in a review except for the use of brief quotations in a book review.

First Printing, 2015

ISBN 13: 978-0-990-99030-7

10 9 8 7 6 5 4 3 2 1

Printed in the United States of America

Conversion of a Pimp: Joseph

(Angela Moore)

Dedication

This book is dedicated to my cousin, Ambur James. Your push forced me to drive, and I'm enjoying the ride. Thanks cuz.

Acknowledgments

Dacia Parker-Crump, thanks for being a great BFF!...

La Tanya Harris, best PR manager out there, thanks my sista...

To my social media peeps; Deandria Rossell, Anita Hall, Kathleene Ann Farrell Corrigan, Shanna Seawood-Chalmers, Crystal Moore, Kelli Lewis-McGruder, Yolanda Wade, Darleana Jones-Campbell, and Author Kimberly Reed (author of "Tryna Squeeze Into My Shoes") - your words of encouragement were more than I expected and I could never thank you ladies enough. My prayer is that MY words will make you laugh, cry and long for more. Thank you, thank you, and thank you!...

Faith Slater, thanks for the feedback!...

Frankie Legge-Vance, it's a beautiful thing when friendships are rekindled...

To my Culver Street Crew, WHOOT WHOOT!...

To my Lovely Lloyd, you helped me stretch my mind to limits I didn't know were obtainable, and for that, I am forever grateful…

Anthony Harrell, friends for life…

Thank you Damone Means for designing the book cover and all of your hard work…

And last but not least, my man Reggie Sykes. No words my friend, no words…

My biggest fan club stems from my immediate family; if I were a dog who started a race with a broken leg, y'all would cheer me on to the finish line! Thanks fam, near and far, much appreciated…

To my parents, Vernon and Linda Ward, SURPRISE! I wrote a book…

To my siblings, I love you guys to pieces… I love you GG…

To my four babies, this is for you…

And to all my other family, friends, and soon to come fans, I say, thank you…

~Matthew 11:28-30~

28 "Come to Me, all you who are weary and burdened, and I will give you rest.

29 Take My yoke upon you and learn from Me, for I am gentle and humble in heart, and you will find rest for your souls.

30 For My yoke is easy and My burden is light."

~JOSEPH~

Preachers ain't shit but pimps in a pulpit. My mama said my daddy was a preacher. When I was a kid, if our electricity was on, I would turn on all them preacher shows and just flick, flick and flick. Hell, I still find myself doing that stupid shit, hardly able to unglue my eyes from the TV, trying to find "daddy." Sometimes I'd flick thru those channels all damn day and night, looking for similarities in those preacher men and me. In my mind I'd be thinking, *which one of these muthafuckas left me with this bitch they call my mama. Her ass didn't do nothing but breathe air that coulda been used by somebody else.* It's because of my mama I see bitches the way I do, as nothing more than a product, merchandise, a means to an end and they've served me very well!

Thanks to my hoes, I live in the best neighborhood with the biggest house on the block on the far West Side of Indianapolis, and if you don't have money, you don't know that there are real people living like this. Drive and float in nothing but the best which includes the best yacht money can buy, and that's with a complete staff. Got my own personal tailor which allows me to dress in nothing but the flyest gear. I pay that nigga well too, making sure I'm his only client. All day every day I rub elbows with the Richie Rich, and because of my bitches, I've become a very wealthy man via the two most powerful instruments used in the world, sex and money.

About 20 years ago I retired my main hoe, Sophia, after she had our 4th kid. Had to sit her ass down to take care of all them damn babies. But, because I'm a businessman first, I

1

told her she had to find a replacement if she wanted to get up off her back, and that's when she sent for her 15 year old cousin from Puerto Rico. Hell, I got Sophia when she was 12, ripe for the pickin'! As soon as she stepped off that bus I sold her a dream and her ass is still waiting for it to come true. She call herself all sanctified now, been going to that church for about seven years. When Sophia made that move, it convinced me all the more that she was stupid. Her ass dun prolly fucked half the congregation, from the preacher on down to the men and women. When she came to me and asked, yeah "ASKED" me if she could start going over there to that church, I looked at her like she was crazy. Shit, made me want to send her ass back out to them streets. She knows how I feel about that bullshit. I don't allow nothing or nobody affiliated with religion up in my house. That's the main reason I like living in a gated community with 24 hour a day security, it stops all those hypocrites at the gate. I didn't even answer her, just walked away. After a while though, I told her she could go, as long as she could still be at my beck and call. And while we were on the subject, I let it be known that she had bet not take any of our kids up in there either, and from what I could tell, she hadn't.

For the most part, Sophia kept her end of the bargain, until I came home one day and saw her in our bedroom on her knees praying. I took off my belt and beat her sanctified ass like there was no tomorrow. "I *slap* THOUGHT *slap* I *slap* TOLD *slap* YOU *slap* NOT *slap* TO *slap* BRING *slap* THAT *slap* SHIT *slap* UP *slap* IN *slap* MY *slap* HOUSE!" Her ass kept right on praying and every time she did I beat dat azz! Over time, she acted like that didn't even faze her, like she wasn't tired of getting the ass whoopins, but shit, I was tired of givin' em. I figured that if she wanted to be deceived, that was her business. I was getting too old for the tug-of-war, and besides, she is the mother of my kids and her trying to hide the bruises when they were around was starting to get old too.

And speaking of kids, we got four. Three boys and one girl, and all them bitches is mine! I ain't bout to take care of no nother nigga's bastards, not after all the shit my own mama put me through. Every time I think back to what my mama did and allowed to happen to me I see red. The Bitch used to tell me "now you gone in there and take care of Mr. John so Mr. John can take of mama." Yeah, The Bitch used to trick me out for her dope, and the sad thing is, that was the only time I saw a smile on her face. She knew that once those niggas was through with me, she was gon get a hit. Hell, sometimes when those grown ass men got finished they wouldn't give her ass shit but uh ass whooping, so hell naw, I ain't bringin' shit that ain't mine up in here!

Although I trained my three boys the strategic art of pimping and getting dat money, I refused to have my daughter end up like her mama or The Bitch by putting her on the block. Besides, I make more money off her brain than I would've on them street corners. At the age of sixteen I sent her ass to college to become a lawyer. Baby girl was smart as hell so I came to the conclusion that there was nobody better than family to take care of family. Hell, it seems like that's been my best investment to date, because whenever one my boys would have to put they foot in somebody's ass because of they paper, daddy and little sis are on speed dial to take care of that shit. Them greenbacks, partna, always bout them greenbacks.

Every move I made when it came to my kids was a strategic one, ensuring that the legacy of the Amos men lives on. And if the streets ain't taught me nothing else, they've taught me that without money, you ain't shit. It's therefore my job to make sure we never run out, and that's by any means necessary, no matter the cost.

With all the kids gone Sophia had nothing to do which was another reason I went ahead and let her go to that church. She didn't do nothing but get on my nerves and shop. It was the getting on my nerves that really sealed the deal. Because of her bored ass we argued all the damn time, all day every day. I'd always have to remind her that she needed to stay in her place, and I'd also threaten to throw her ass back on them corners if she didn't. I don't know what made her think she could go ham on me, especially when she knows how I get down. And ain't no way her stupid ass didn't know that when I was fuckin' her, I was fuckin' all my other hoes too. I guess she thought she was special because she was the mother of my kids. *Bitch, please, you besta man the fuck down!* She was always going too far thinkin' I wasn't gon notice her sneaky ass snooping through my shit. I shut that down real quick and let it be known that I don't let a muthafuckin' thang slip past me. Guess she dun forgot her position since she up in the big house; I therefore commenced to beat that ass to wake her up from her short-term memory loss.

Now, when Sophia had first started going over to that church, I laid down the rules and it just so happened that there was one I forgot to mention, but to me, that was uh unspoken rule, one I shouldn't even hafta open my mouth to speak on.

One Sunday I was in the den, flicking thru channels, with the volume on mute, looking for that nigga, when Sophia brought one of them "holy rollers" over and introduced her to me as her "sister in Christ." As soon as Sophia looked in my eyes, she knew she had fucked up. I could see her pleading with me to not go monkey on her ass, so I didn't, which was torture in itself. I was cool but couldn't wait till that bitch left. After she bounced I called Sophia into our bedroom and when she walked in, she saw the belt in my hand. She knew what time it was and got butt naked; I beat that ass like she stole something. I don't know why she thought what she did was ok. I suppose she thought it was smooth sailing because she would always see me scrolling through the channels, with the volume on mute, looking for that nigga that look like me. Naw sweetie, this ain't that. While I beat her down I told her that she had bet not bring none of those hypocrites up in my space no more, and she didn't!

The Bitch they call my mama died about four years ago and there wasn't no love lost on my part. Since Sophia wasn't trickin' no mo', her and The Bitch had built a pretty tight relationship. It seemed like every time I looked up Sophia would be hightailin' it out the house going to break with her ass. In my mind I would be thinkin' *birds of a feather, flock, flock, flock.* I found out The Bitch was sick when I walked in on Sophia trying to convince one of our kids to go see her ass before it was too late. I snatched that phone outta Sophia's hand and threw that shit up against the wall. I gave her a look that said *yo ass gon be in the grave before her if you keep fuckin' with me!* She was always in the middle trying to put cement on a relationship where the cinder blocks were forever shattered, and I wasn't having that!

I remember Sophia coming home one day saying The Bitch wanted to see me. When those words rolled off her tongue, I wanted to take my thumb and forefinger and pull out her damn trachea. I stood there and closed my eyes for a long time, trying not to lose my damn mind. When I opened them, I looked at her like she didn't have no damn head. I then asked her why she thought it was ok to even approach me bout that bullshit. Like going to see the person who tricked me out and called me "muthafucka" all the damn time was to be disregarded, like somebody accidentally poppin' a balloon. The Bitch said that shit so much I thought that was my real name! "Muthafucka, get yo nasty ass in here!" "Muthafucka, go get me some damn Newport's, or muthafucka, I need you to go grocery shopping," which actually meant, I needed to go down to the corner store and steal some food if I wanted to eat. Shit, sometimes I'd be so hungry I resorted to eating toilet paper to get full, if we had any, and usually we didn't. Or "Muthafucka, shut that damn door, you ain't paying no damn bills up in here!" In my mind I'd be thinking, *Yes the hell I do, I pay all them bitches with my ass.* Naw, I told her to go tell The Bitch good riddance, and that I'll see her ass in hell.

About two weeks after that Sophia asked me if we could talk, said The Bitch told her to tell me that she was sorry and that she loved me. Oh really? Well put a nigga on ice cause I ain't even tryin' to hear that! Ya see, about a year before The Bitch got real sick, Sophia started pickin' her up for church, so in my eyes you just saying what the pimp in the pulpit told you to say, getting that soul right before you meet ya maker kinda shit. Naw, it's going to take more than that for me to forgive The Bitch for fucking up my life. I'm not the one. About a month later I heard Sophia in our bedroom crying, and that's how I found out The Bitch was dead, oh well! The world's a better place because of it.

In my eyes, Sophia has always been weak-minded, and when she came home one night after Bible study and told me that she'd learned that her name means "wisdom", my ideology of her stupidity was confirmed. I had been in the den, flicking through channels with the volume on mute, looking for that nigga when she'd walked in and told me that shit. I looked up from my TV, and for a couple minutes I didn't say shit. When I couldn't stand looking at her dumb ass no more I said, "The only wise choice you ever made in yo simple ass life was getting with me." I watched her joy crumble as she dropped her head. To keep fucking wit her, I asked her what she was always praying for, told her that the God she was praying to must not be listening to her because her ass was always somewhere hemmed up on her knees. She looked up at me, and with tears running down her face said, "You." That shit sent a damn chill down my spine. I recovered real quick and just looked at her. I shook my head and told her she needed to be praying for her damn self, while she was up in that church listening to them false teachings them niggas was whispering in her ear. Telling her shit that don't make no crazy sense. Her head was still down when she turned around and started heading for the stairs, and that's when I heard her say, real soft like, "I got the whole church praying for you."

I couldn't believe my damn ears. I yelled, "Come here, Sophia!" I know she thought I was about to give her ass a beat down, but I didn't want to beat her physically, naw, I didn't want to do that, I just wanted to give her a little knowledge on how the real world worked. When she was in front of me, I stood up, and as I went to put both my hands on her shoulders she flinched. I squeezed them bitches real hard and then yanked her closer to me. I looked in her sad, ass downcast eyes and said, "Now look at me! I know you all up in that church stuff, right, but #1, there ain't no God, and #2, if for one second I did give the whole God thing some thought, I'd like to be the first to let you know that He don't answer no prayers, cause He sho in the hell didn't answer none of mine when I was praying as grown ass men were fucking me!" I shoved her away and told her to go get my shit together and to start my bath water.

When I went up a little later I heard some sniffling sounds coming from one of the guest bedrooms. I walked to the door, cracked it opened and there she was, kneeling next to the bed, praying and crying. I didn't even have the energy to beat her ass, which I still did when the moment struck me. I just closed the door, went into my bathroom and got undressed. I hit the button on my surround sound, and turned that bitch all the way up blasting Tupac. I fired up my joint, and with my glass of cognac Sophia had made in hand, eased into the tub. If Sophia wanted to throw up prayers to a throne where nobody reigned, I didn't have no problem with that, she just needed to keep my name out her mouth! Hell, I had my own throne, and at that moment I was soaking in it. I took a toke off my bud, picked up the remote to my 96 inch, and started flicking through channels, with the volume on mute, looking for that nigga that look like me.

When Sophia's ass wasn't where I needed her to be, I could look out of the living room window and bam! I'd see her in her car reading her Bible, and sometimes for hours. That was one of the first rules I laid down when she started going to fraternize with the fakers, no church paraphernalia or nothing religious up in my crib. And when I said nothing, that's what the hell I meant, NOTHING! No Bibles, no CDs, no gospel stations, no tapes, no tracts, no pamphlets, no newsletters, NONE! She ain't never formed her mouth to ask to go on one of those suck up all ya money mission trips either, she wasn't that stupid and knew how I got down. She also knew not to come at me about the kids going to nobodies nothing! For what? So that they could be molested by the preacher or one of those deceiving ass deacons? She wasn't going to no Catholic church but I didn't give a fuck, they all wanted the same thing, money and sex. My kids were out of the house by the time she started going, but I didn't give a damn because it was grown ass men who were up in my ass every other day. Naw, leave my kids out that shit, grown or not. I will say this though; since she's been going to see her new pimp and his hoes, we hardly ever argue. I'm flicking through the channels, with the volume on mute, looking for that nigga.

I was always watching Sophia's ass, just waiting for her to mess up. Waiting for her to give me a reason to bust her upside her head, but she rarely did. She'd been doing good since I gave her a little freedom. Sometimes she'd be walking around the house with her headphones on, and I know she done eased some religious shit up on that mp3 player she be listening to. She be prancing around the crib humming and singing and shit. One day she got a little louder than usual. I was in the den flicking through channels, with the volume on mute, looking for that nigga, when I thought I'd heard the radio on. That shit was sounding good then a mug. I followed the sound and it led me to the kitchen. When I walked in I saw Sophia washing dishes and soon realized that the sound was coming from her. She had her back to me and was blowin'. I couldn't believe what I was hearing. That shit was so fly I thought her mp3 had come disconnected. I just stood there watching and listening because I had never heard no shit like that. When she turned around and saw me staring; she dropped her head and shut her mouth real fast. I didn't say nothing, just walked away to go flick through channels. We never talked about that incident, but I never told her she couldn't sing no more either. She had a nice voice, and I did like to hear it, and that's the only reason I let that one slide. What's messed up is the fact that we been together all these years and I didn't even know she could sing. I guess her ass ain't had nothing to sing about till now.

I give Sophia 25 g's a week for an allowance. She's a damn good mother and did good with our kids. I still got them bank statements in my name though, and know where every dime goes. Sophia mighta been a hoe, but when she came to the big house, her ass learned real quick how to put a dent in a nigga's pockets. In the beginning she spent every penny she got, but mostly on the kids. She always used her coins for "extra shit" she wanted them to have, *whatever*! She had a weekly budget that included the kids' private school, clothes and food, anything left over was to go back into the bank, but once the kids started leaving, I gave her a little more leeway when it came to herself. The whole personal tailor thing didn't sit well with her. She wanted to be up close and personal with everything she set her eyes on so that's what she did, shop, shop and mo shopping. The whole shopping thing got old real quick, and because she didn't trust too many people, she started getting mighty lonely, and it was at that time I told her she could go and start regularly exchanging spit with the fakers. She didn't have a lot of friends and the ones she did have she didn't trust, until she started going to that church. One day I was reading her bank statement when I saw that the church was the reason her bank balance hadn't changed. I just shook my head. Every week she was putting half that shit in the pimp's hat, paying for that nigga to sneak his sidepiece out the house so he can take her to a movie and dinner. I know that if I'd told Sophia to stop she would've, but it wasn't even that deep. I just knew that if she saw a mink she wanted for 75 g's, she had bet not come at me with an outstretched hand. Because if she did, I'd have to tell her she had a new pimp over at that church and to divert all her wants in his direction because I didn't have a damn thang for her.

One night I took Sophia to dinner at one of the elite restaurants on the outskirts of town, and lo and behold, who should come up to our table? None other than the pimp himself. Her ass got all happy and excited, jumped up and hugged his ass like she had been starving for one. I didn't even look their way. I did listen to their conversation though and heard her pimp say he wanted to thank the both of us for the generous contribution we gave to the church so that him and his wife could celebrate their anniversary. In my mind I thought *I ain't gave y'all shit!* His ass went on to say that although their anniversary was three months ago, that night was the safest time for them to have a night on the town, said they couldn't be going in and out too much because of his immune system. I was eating the whole time they were standing there, didn't want to give them any space to ask me how I was doing or to come visit their church. I wasn't trying to hear none of that. I could see them out the corner of my eyes though, and he wasn't nothing like I be seeing on those TV shows. He was all thin with a mask over his nose and mouth. I heard the hiss of uh oxygen tank and thought, *damn his ass is messed up*. I don't know what I was expecting but it sure in the hell wasn't that. They said their parting words without any foul plays, which was cool by me. I had been waiting on they asses to give me a reason to go there, but they hadn't. The same quiet way they came to our table, was the same quiet way they left. Once they were gone I looked up at Sophia and her ass was happy as hell. She had been in a sullen mood when we got there because during our commute, I'd made fun of her ass for giving all her money to her new pimp. She didn't say a word, just continued looking out of the window as I laughed at her simple ass. But while looking at her from across our dinner table, I realized, that as a fellow pimp, I had never put that kind of a smile on her face.

We drove home from the restaurant in silence. Me in my world thinking about some shit two of my son's had gotten they his asses into, and her in her world thinking about what her dumb ass thinks about. When we got into the house, I went to the den and started flicking through channels, with the volume on mute, looking for that nigga, while she put on her headphones and started prancing around the house, singing with her beautiful voice.

Later that night, my ass had started noddin' when I heard the doorbell ringing. Sophia was in another room playing her loud ass music so I figured she hadn't heard. She musta had a delayed reaction because as I was opening the door, she was coming from the kitchen, drying her hands on a dishtowel. All I saw were blue and red lights with two men in uniform standing on my front porch. The first thing I thought was *who the fuck let them in? They asses are just as bad as the hypocrites.* My phone started to ring and so did Sophia's, but we didn't pay them no mind. The theatrical scene playing out in front of me started feeling like I was in a damn dream, because before I knew it, shit was happening in slow muthafuckin' motion. Sophia walking into the entryway, the men in uniform talking, the phones poppin' off like popcorn and those blue and red lights molesting my home. The shit was getting slower and slower until my ears started ringing because I knew I hadn't heard what the fuck I'd just heard! Then there was a soft "what?" beside me. I turned and saw Sophia taking out her other earplug, and watched her face contort into horror. I stepped to her just in time to catch her before she hit the floor, and watched as a lone tear slid down her flawless, chocolate face. I thought, *Them niggas dun picked the wrong muthafuckin' family, and some heads is bout to be smashed!*

~SOPHIA~

I know he hates to see me pray, and no matter how many times he beats me, I ain't stopping. I've come from a very dark and bad place so I refuse to allow him or anybody else to snatch away my joy. I'm so grateful for God's mercy and love! Every time I think about what I've been through in this thing called life, I want to cry. I've had a hard one, and I know when people look at me, all they see is the stuff, because I got plenty of it, Joseph makes sure of that. That man has been in my life since I was twelve years old and stuck on stupid. I was so naïve at that age. I didn't even know how to change a pad, he had to teach me, along with some other things that would turn my life upside down, because all that I'd obtained, I got the hard way, on my knees, and on my back.

With the life I've lived you would think that I grew up on the wrong side of the tracks, but that ain't even true. My family got money, and plenty of it. My dad was active in politics, with his snow-white queen parading along his side. My mother died when I was two, so The Witch, a title I gave her, had been the only active mother figure I'd known. The name title might sound childish, but it's one she's earned. She never let a day slip by without whispering immature phrases into my ear, a small reminder of her disapproval of my skin color. I was an innocent child and couldn't understand what I'd done to merit such hatred, but would soon learn that nothing needed to be done; my mere existence was enough.

My mom was black, my dad Puerto Rican, and I am the product of young love. My dad never let me forget how pretty my mother was, and made sure every person who walked into our home knew it as well. Pictures of my mom were like pieces of furniture, everywhere, even the bathroom. The woman I've come to know through the fond memories of others was the victim of a drive-by shooting, and her senseless death left my dad numb. He couldn't comprehend how someone who was trying to save a community could end up being nothing more than a statistic via the hands of the people they were trying to save. In reality, it was because of my mom that my dad got into politics. In that sector, he's kept her memory alive by fighting for stricter gun laws and holding lawmakers to a higher standard when prosecuting the heartless behavior of others. Although he worked tirelessly for change, he was consumed with grief, and that combination was the perfect concoction for an opportunist to sink their fangs into his jugular.

I have always called kids "the silent victims" when it comes to life. They see and hear everything, suck it all in like a sponge, but know how to keep grownup secrets. I was five when my dad remarried, and I was acutely aware of the spirit of cunning his new wife had. While around the public and my dad, she was as sweet as honey, but in private her ass was sneaky, deceptive and violent. Because my dad was always campaigning or trying to pass a law, I was left with The Witch, and the things I saw that woman do made me long for the beauty of my mother more and more. I recall listening to her on the phone talking to her OBGYN, trying to figure out why she had yet to get pregnant. She was yelling and screaming at that man like he was the Almighty and had the powerful gift of conception. I suppose I was the one deceived because the next thing I knew, The Witch and my daddy were getting married, and eight months later I had a little brother, then ten months after that another brother, then a year after him, a little sister. Her conniving butt knew she had sealed the deal by having my daddy's babies and boldly let it be known that she wasn't going nowhere.

Angela Moore

Anytime she had an opportunity, The Witch would make it her business to let me know I was the odd child out. That woman hated me with a passion that superseded anything I had ever encountered! It may have been because every time she looked at one of my mom's pictures, all she had to do was look down at me to see the same face, just on a smaller body. My dad had refused to remove any of my mom's photos from the walls, even after he remarried, and somebody had to pay for that bold level of disrespect, me. She taunted me daily by calling me derogatory names, like nigga child, darkie and buckwheat. Who in the hell does that to a five-year old? What kind of insane adult torments a baby because of their own self-image problems? Little did I know...name calling was child's play when dealing with an attention starved devil like The Witch.

Every time one of my siblings was brought home from the hospital, I noticed that they had fair skin with straight hair, whereas I was dark with curly hair, no big thing to me. I was just happy to have a new baby brother or sister. But not so for The Witch, in her warped thought process, my complexion and hair were the two things that triggered her pores to see the resentment. In her mind, if I didn't exist, she'd have the picture perfect family. It didn't look good to be standing on a political podium with a drop of chocolate, other than my dad, in the midst. She would therefore try to use her body to shield me from the world, which prompted me to draw closer to my father, stand front and center with him, and use his presence as my protection. Because I sensed her determination to make me disappear, I'd take ahold of my dad's hand and hold on to it real tight, as if my life depended on it, because it did.

The first time I knew her ass was extra evil was when my dad had thrown a campaign party at our house for his reelection. I don't know why, but for some reason, while minding my own business, I looked over my shoulder and saw The Witch and a white man looking dead at me as they spoke in hushed voices. Although I was seven, I knew something wasn't right, so for the remainder of the evening I stuck to my dad like glue. That was the only time I felt safe. While standing beside him, it was very comforting to feel his hand on my shoulder as he gently rubbed it back and forth while speaking with his guest. It took me back to a time when it was just the two of us, when our life was quiet and simple, moments I dearly missed. Throughout the night The Witch would slyly ease her way over to us, trying to pry me from my dad's embrace. Shooooot! She had to be outta her mind to think that her forked tongue could persuade me to leave my safe haven, not in a million years. Once she realized I wasn't budging, I could feel the venom of her fake smile seep into my veins as she walked away. But her eyes, her eyes screamed, "I'll teach you."

The party had started winding down, and although I knew it was past my bedtime, I stood by my dad's side until he bid his last guest goodbye. After he'd shut and locked the door for the night, I'd tried, to no avail, to talk him into letting me staying up a little longer, and when I ignored his reasoning, I was two seconds away from getting a royal beat down. It was weird, but somehow my seven-year old intuition told me something just wasn't right. I didn't know what it was, but I knew it was very bad.

I reluctantly went to my room, trying my hardest not to fall asleep, but eventually sleep won out. I can't recall the time of night, but I do recall feeling pressure on my bed and a hand going under my nightgown. That's when my ass hopped up, but I was pushed back down with a hand over my mouth. I started kicking, screaming and fighting, but was no match for a grown ass man on a mission. Out of the corner of my eye I could see The Witches silhouette in the darkness, and no matter how hard I cried I knew she'd die and go to hell before she'd lift her porcelain foot to come help me. I could not believe what was happening to me, and in actuality, I didn't know what was happening. I was a baby; I wasn't supposed to know! All it took was one sad, cold night for me to be transformed from a child into a woman, in a matter of minutes.

That wickedness went on for five years, and only ceased because of me. The Witch had me feeling like I was living in a real live Cinderella book, except in my story I had no glass slipper and no one to come rescue me. I was at my wit's end, and just couldn't take it anymore. By then my body had really started developing, with men taking notice of every change. The sad thing is, every man noticed but the man I wanted to notice, my dad. It had been years since my mom had been gone, and years since he'd been remarried, but my dad was still living in the presence of a time gone by. The Witch may have had my dad in the physical, but my mom still held his heart, and that was the driving force behind his accomplishments. And although I didn't want to admit it, in reality, neither one of us had him. My dad was kinda old-school in his thought process when it came to family. Wife stays with the kids, husband makes the living and provides for his family, so that's how we lived, and because of that I was basically invisible, along with my pain.

I was twelve but I wasn't stupid. Being around The Witch had taught me some survival skills that kicked in when I needed them most.

In preparation for my great escape, I stole as much cash and as many jewels as I could, and then hit the road. I didn't know where I was going and didn't care as long as I was out of that hellhole. While in the streets, I would watch the news on my cell phone and see my dad on TV pleading with the whole state to lookout for me. *Oh, so now I exist?* I was so over the dramatics, and by then, my own heart had become numb. I figured that if nobody else was going to make sure I was safe, I'd have to do it myself. Little did I know I'd just left hell, only to walk willing into the arms of Satan himself.

I was running out of money, and being twelve with no real street knowledge didn't help my cause. I was robbed, raped and beaten by the other alley cats who knew the ropes of the streets better than I did. It seemed that no matter where I turned my situation was becoming bleaker and bleaker. I had to find a solution, so in my young mind I thought that if I left those tragedies and disappointments behind, I'd be able to start fresh, with a clean slate in a new state. I therefore set the wheels of my destiny into motion, and would one day question whose venom was deadliest, Joseph's or The Witch's, because they were both lifeguards to the lake of fire.

With my funds almost depleted, I bought the cheapest ticket I could afford. Although I was twelve, I didn't look it, so purchasing a ticket was easy as cake, with Indiana being my chosen destination. I hit that paved road of destiny with childish dreams and immature thoughts hoping for a better tomorrow, but ended up with calloused knees and broken dreams, in a relationship with the devil.

I got off that bus and there he was, Lucifer himself, waiting on a child like me. I didn't know where to go or what to do so I went into the bus terminal, sat down, and looked around. What does a twelve year old know about starting over? I didn't even know what street I was on. I was a complete mess, but welcomed the unknown more than what was known. But one thing was for certain - I couldn't go back. If I had, I would've only suffocated myself with sorrow. And then there he was, Joseph. He saw me on that bench looking lost and came to the rescue. With a smooth tongue he asked, "Are you lost, little girl? You waiting on somebody?" I said absolutely nothing, looking everywhere but in his eyes. He kept picking, "I'll take care of you" and picking "I got everything you need" and picking "I won't hurt you" until I broke. I looked into his eyes and that's when he had me, a little black girl lost. He coaxed me to his car, promised me he'd take care of me. Said he had a nice warm bed and food, all for free. In time I'd realize that I'd just sold my soul to the devil, and that I was to never, ever, take anything Joseph said to me literally.

Being with Joseph was like being in the military, all mind games. What the government does is get you away from everybody by putting you in an environment where it's just you, the other new recruits, and them. In basic training they feed you real good; steak, lobster, salmon, big healthy salads with all the extra toppings, with as many sides as you like and plenty, plenty water, they don't want their butterflies getting dehydrated. But, you have a certain amount of time to eat and you learn real fast, get it down or it gets left. And don't forget to drink your water; they don't want their butterflies getting dehydrated. They yell and scream at you but it's only to build your character and make you a better person. And they give you plenty, plenty water, because they don't want their butterflies getting dehydrated. They have a real nice graduation ceremony, and allow you to invite all your family and friends so everyone can see how good they've been treating you. And with any first time experience away from home, if you don't have family, somebody else's adopts you on the spot and they encourage you by whispering in your ear, "Make sure you drink plenty of water, they don't like their butterflies getting dehydrated." And then after all the pleasantries, they introduce you to what the government is really about - themselves. They've just accomplished one of the greatest feats in human history, deceiving you with mind games, convincing you that what they have to offer will exceed your wildest dreams, and as they snatch away your mind, they give you plenty of water, because they don't want their butterflies getting dehydrated. They snatch all that good food away too, replace it with rations, but you still get plenty of water, they can't let that butterfly get dehydrated. They're gracious enough to give you a role to play; in winter, spring, summer and fall and reward you if you are successful, with plenty more water, they can't let their butterfly get dehydrated. You still get to keep some of the benefits from basic training though, food, shelter and clothing or so you think, because what they don't tell you is when you get your first paycheck all that stuff is deducted. But, they give you plenty of water; they can't let their butterfly get dehydrated. And if you do real well, they let you relax a little and let you become a recruiter. And I was Joseph's best one.

Joseph had trained me well. I was a quick learner and that allowed me to move up in rank real fast. Initially, in my young dumb mind I thought I was the only one, and was crushed when I met the other fifteen and realized I was just one of many. He had a total of twelve regular girls and I was lucky number thirteen and the youngest. He didn't allow me around the other hoes until he'd broken me in with his street smarts. But as soon as the introductions began, I could feel the jealousy. Joseph had warned me ahead of time by telling me, "If them bitches say one wayward word to you, let me know. You bout to take money out they pockets which means I'ma hafta put my foot in they ass." And he wasn't lying. When I was getting dressed to go meet a John, the head hoe, Phoebe, got me while my back was turned. Joseph wasn't paying her as much attention as he was paying me. That blew her skirt up and she was not having that! She beat me so bad, Joseph had to get one of his street doctors to take care of me for a whole month. The other girls were helping with my recovery too. They told me that Joseph had made Phoebe put in more work because she had fucked up major dollars. I didn't give a damn what was going on, I just wanted to get better so that my pain would go away.

Joseph came to see me every day and I felt real special until he said, "Now look here, we need to make sure you get everything you need and get that pretty skin back to that pretty color. And make sure you drink plenty water, we don't want **MY** butterfly getting dehydrated." That statement broke my stupid ass heart. I don't know why I thought my butterfly was special; I guess I was just really hoping he'd see me differently than other men.

Once I was back on my game, Joseph pulled me to the side and said, "Now, you know you special. Right?" I rolled my eyes and thought *whatever nigga!* He continued by saying, "And because you so special I'ma pull you up in rank, you gon be my recruiter now, baby. I'ma need you to hit them streets cause we in need of a few more butterflies and you the perfect one to get 'em for me, and I need 'em young too."

I wanted to ask him, "Why me?" but I wasn't trying to see that big black fist coming toward my eye on a day to day. I experienced that brutal side of Joseph three months after he lured me from that bus station. He'd wanted me to wear a purple leather outfit for a customer who chose what color he wanted to see his girls in, and like any twelve year old I started whining but before I could get a complete 'why' out, he hit me so hard in my face I actually saw real live stars.

He told me, "Bitch, don't you ever question shit I tell you to do again!" He didn't have to tell me twice. I did exactly what he said the way he said it. So I took my butt out to them streets and brought him his young butterflies. I don't know why it didn't occur to me that that was Phoebe's job, and that as soon as I got better; nobody had seen or talked to her again. I silently thanked Phoebe for the heads up, wherever she was, because in my heart I knew her lungs wasn't breathin' no kinda air.

When Joseph broke me in, by tasting the product, I would always have my eyes closed when he was on top of me. Did the same thing I did with that white man, went to another place, and had been doing that for years. Then one day, out the blue, Joseph said, "Open them damn eyes," and I closed them tighter. I felt his hands go around my neck and start to squeeze. My eyes popped open then! With him on top of me, and his hands around my neck, I had no choice but to look into his eyes, and wanted to weep, not for myself, but for him. All I saw was hatred and such profound sadness. They were void of hope or anything real, just dead. As he started to squeeze tighter I felt something wet fall on my face and that's when I noticed the tears, his, not mine. I didn't know what the hell that was all about but what I did know was that I couldn't breathe so I started fighting for my life. I guess somebody musta heard the struggle because as I was passing out I heard Joseph yell, "Don't you ever put yo muthafuckin' hands on me again, bitch!" **SLAP**!

I didn't see Joseph for a whole month after that. He sent my assignments through the girls but didn't touch me or come near me for thirty damn days! My ass got real scared. Joseph's mind was always all over the place and with him being M.I.A. I just knew he was plotting my demise. I'd seen him weak and he didn't like that. By this time I'd been with him for three years and still didn't know anybody anywhere other than other hoes and tricks. I'd learned many things in those three years while with that man, and survival was one of them. I know it's hard to believe but it wasn't until that moment that I could actually appreciate the scheming of The Witch. I wouldn't have thought in a million years that she'd ever have character traits that I would come use and to hold on to. While growing up, I'd watched as she'd manipulated, lied and fought to seal her fate, and dammit, it was time for me to seal mine.

When I met Joseph I thought he was much older than I was, but later found out that he had me by seven lousy years, although he'd already lived three lifetimes. In spite of the small age gap, I always let Joseph think I was young and dumb. Hell, that's part of the game when you a hoe, always make ya pimp look a whole lot bigger than what he is. Don't get me wrong, I did fear Joseph, I had better had, but I was also a survivor and when dealing with the oldest profession in the world, a lot of traditions of the trade have been handed down from hoe to hoe. We are a family of women in the struggle trying to make sure we #1 made our pimp the happiest pimp on the block and #2 stay alive long enough to enjoy a few crumbs from the royalties. You've gotta remember, Joseph was all I had, he was my everything, I had absolutely nobody else in the world and I was not about to be kicked to the curb because of some damn pride. Heck, I had men pay good money to lick and kiss my damn knees, so nigga please! It was time for Sophia to start looking out for Sophia.

When Joseph finally got over himself and started touching me again, survival mode went into full effect! I'm fifteen, lonely, sad, miserable, abandoned, weak, and vulnerable; the list went on and on. I sit that shit to the side real quick, now I'm fifteen, and survival mode is in overdrive and I wasn't slowing down for no speed bumps.

Joseph is on top of me when he says, "Open them damn eyes, Sophia." I open them, wide. We look in each other's eyes. We look in each other's eyes. We look into each other's eyes. Then something happens to my butterfly and both our eyes are closed tight. *Yesss, Joseph! I know he loves me,* something happens to my butterfly. *Oh, Yesss! I know he loves me,* his hands are squeezing my hands, something happens to my butterfly. *Please. Yesss! I know he loves me,* I start to squeeze his hands, something happens to my butterfly. *Joseph, oh Joseph. Yesss! I know he loves me,* I open my eyes, something happens to my butterfly. *Yesss baby, yesss! I know he loves me,* his eyes are closed, something's happening to my butterfly. *YESSS! I! KNOW! HE! LOVES! ME!* I say, as something's happening to my butterfly, "Open yo muthafuckin' eyes, nigga!" He opens them and for the first time in my life, my butterfly is hydrated, and his ass cain't get enough of my water.

Three months later a hoe is pregnant, she has a baby boy and names him Jacob. Two months later, a hoe is pregnant; she has a baby boy and names him Jonathan. Seven months later, a hoe is pregnant and she has another boy, and names him Jude. Three months later, a hoe is pregnant and she has her beautiful baby girl and she names her Shalom…*Now who's the pimp…nicca?*

~JOSEPH~

After I caught Sophia, I carried her to the den and laid her on the couch. My phone was still blowing up so I answered out of frustration as I led the men in blue into my kitchen. It was my baby girl Shalom and she was hysterical. The police were trying to ask me questions as I was trying to listen to her; I held my finger up to them and listened intently to what Shalom was saying. I felt the veins in my forehead and neck start to pulsate as my knees felt like they were going to fold from up under me. I ended the call by telling her, "Don't tell they asses shit" then looked at the police. Their lips were moving but I didn't hear a damn thang they said. Out of the corner of my eye I saw Sophia walking into the kitchen and told her to go get our coats. As I watched her retreat, I told the men in blue that I wanted my boys under aliases with guards at their hospital doors. They told me that all victims of violent crimes get aliases but didn't know if guards would be available. As Sophia was walking in, we all started heading for the front door. I took out my phone and got in touch with my main man, James, and told him that I wanted some of the crew placed outside of my boys' rooms and that I knew the streets were talkin', so I therefore needed the know what the fuck they were sayin'. He told me it was already taken care of and I hung up. His ass was a talker his damn self and I wasn't tryin' to hear nothin' else he had to say. We hopped into our separate rides as the police escorted us to the hospital. Other than Sophia's moaning in the passenger seat, there was total silence in the car, but I heard a whole lotta voices in my head and what they were whispering to me was going to make some niggas wish they'd never been born.

As we walked through the Emergency Room doors, I could see the top of my baby girl's head. She was surrounded by the police who were asking her a thousand and one questions. I told those boys to man the fuck down and that they needed to direct all questions in the direction of our attorney. When that sea of blue parted and I laid eyes on my baby girl my whole damn mind went black. I couldn't believe what my eyes were beholding. She had glass stuck in her hair that was held in place by her brother's blood. Although she was wearing an all-black outfit, I could still see blotches of dark spots throughout her clothes, which let me know what she was covered in. Her left arm was wrapped in an ace bandage and she had gauze on her left cheek. Just as our attorney walked in she saw me and sprinted into my arms. I held baby girl so tight I thought I'd break her in two. As Shalom was weeping I turned around to look for Sophia. Her ass was stuck on stupid. She was standing in front of the ER door with her eyes on our only daughter who had the blood of her brothers all over her. I turned back around to Shalom and left Sophia's ass standing right where she was while trying to decipher what baby girl was saying. Out of nowhere I felt what seemed like a thousand knives being thrust into my back. "YOU NO GOOD FOR NOTHING MUTHAFUCKA! LOOK WHAT YOU DID TO MY BOYS! LOOK WHAT YOU DID TO MY BAAABIIIES!" I looked over my shoulder and saw that it was Sophia's ass and she looked damn near possessed. She was beating me down with her pointy ass heeled stilettos and that shit hurt like hell. I turned all the way around and grabbed both her arms with one hand then I slapped her ass so hard with the other that she hit the floor with a thud. She bounced back up like a rubber band and came at me again. I slapped that ass right back down. She had streams of tears running down her face as she hopped back up and came at me a third time. I was just about to put my fist in her eye when Shalom blocked the blow by running to Sophia. I saw Shalom flinch as she tried to block her mother from gettin' to me. We had an audience but I didn't give a damn. I told Shalom to step aside and when she did Sophia came at me like a raging bull and I let her have her way. She punched and screamed and screamed and punched. I let her get what she had in her out until she scratched me on my damn neck. I grabbed her face with my left hand and squeezed real hard. I looked into her broken eyes, bent down and gave her a gentle kiss, then pushed her ass to the floor as I went looking for my boys.

~SOPHIA~

Why am I in the den? Joseph never lets anyone into this room. And why in the world is my head hurting so badly?
And then I remember. I start to freaking remember! I pulled out my phone and started making calls, first to my minister, then to my sisters in Christ. It was time for the saints to send up prayers on behalf of me and my family, and we needed them bad! I had to make those calls fast, while at the same time whispering and suppressing my anguish. I'd heard voices so I knew Joseph was close and I didn't want him walking in on me talking to God's people. After the last call was made I followed the sound of the voices and quietly walked into the kitchen. I saw those men in uniform, and then broke down. Joseph told me to get our coats, and when I turned to do so, I heard him tell the policemen that he wanted guards at our boys' doors. Hearing him say that caused me to run like a bat outta hell towards the entryway closet. I could barely see where I was going because the tears were coming too fast. I swung the closet door open so wide it hit my head and I thought I was going to blackout. I had to stand there for a few seconds to gather myself. My head had already been pounding so that brutal impact didn't help. I slowly rubbed my right temple with my right hand as I reached in and grabbed our coats with my left. *Oh my goodness!* I felt like my brain was splitting in two. I ran back toward the kitchen as the men were coming out and damn

near pushed everybody down trying to get to our car. That head of mine was going to have to wait, there were more pressing issues at hand.

As we were walking out the door, I heard Joseph giving the policemen a more precise list of the things he wanted, and then I listened as he called that snake in the grass James to tell him to make sure our boys were looked after. As we were driving away from our mansion, I was staring out the window looking at nothing as the tears ran down my face.

My babies! My babies! My baaabiiies! My mind was all over the place as I started getting an excruciating headache. Joseph hung up the phone and sat silently, listening to my moaning. As I thought about what might be, I started feeling like I was going to be sick. I prayed I wouldn't because the police were in front of us doing 90 mph so I knew Joseph wasn't gonna stop for nothing and that I'd end up visiting my babies with vomit all over me and Lord knows I didn't want that. Once we got to the Emergency Room entrance, I followed as Joseph was led into the Emergency Room foyer then stopped dead in my tracks. It was like my mind was playing tricks on me because I saw Joseph at our front door, the blue and red lights, Joseph running towards me as I blacked out. The police in our kitchen, and then I saw my babies. I saw when they were in the cradle, in my arms as I quietly sang to them, at the playground playing with their friends, at recitals, in plays, at their graduations, walking into our home giving me kisses and long hugs, bringing me birthday gifts. *MY BABIES, MY BABIES, MY BABIES!* And then I saw red. I looked up and saw my gorgeous Shalom, my pretty baby with all that blood on her, so much damn BLOOD! And her pretty, chocolate face. *What's wrong with my baby's damn FACE? Is her foot bandaged too? How did her foot get messed up?*

And then I snapped. I saw Joseph's big broad back, took off my shoes and charged. I had tunnel vision and the next thing I knew I was hitting and cursing and cursing and hitting. "YOU NO GOOD FOR NOTHING MUTHAFUCKA! LOOK WHAT YOU DID TO MY BOYS! LOOK WHAT YOU DID TO MY BAAABIIIES!" Then SLAP! I hit that floor hard as hell, but didn't care. I screamed, "IS THAT ALL YOU GOT, NIGGA?" I was up again, charging and hitting and cussing, "YOU BASTARD! YOOOOU BASTARD!" SLAP! I felt like I was flying in the air before I hit that floor, and the impact was just as painful as the first. "YOU HIT LIKE A BIIITCH!" Then I was up again, swinging at the air and cursing until my beautiful Shalom came between us. All I heard were bells ringing in my ears, but the ringing stopped when she stepped aside and that's when I charged that ass again. I had dropped my stilettos, and was hitting Joseph with all my might until he grabbed my face and squeezed. I guess I was in a blind rage because I opened my eyes and looked into his. His eyes said, *"I'm sorry, baby."* He placed the most soft and gentle kiss on my swollen lips, then pushed me to the floor.

~JOSEPH~

I saw they butts as soon as I walked through the ER doors but I had more important matters to attend to than entertaining they asses. I told the nurse at the front desk that I needed my boys' room numbers. She said my youngest son, Jude, was still in surgery and hadn't been given a room yet, but led me to my other boys' rooms. At my request, Jacob and Jonathan were located next to each other and as she escorted me to the elevator, my mind was all over the place trying to prepare myself for what was to come. We got off on the third floor and that's when I saw a couple of cats posted outside my boys' doors. I gave them both head nods then went into the room closest to me, the one the nurse led me to. When I walked through that door, I couldn't even tell which son it was. Whoever the hell it was, was bandaged all up and had tubes comin' out of every orifice. As I walked closer I saw long wavy hair laid out on his pillow like a black halo, and knew that it was my oldest boy Jacob. He was real vain when it came to his dome and wouldn't get his hair cut for nothin' or nobody. When I finally made it to his bedside, I couldn't believe my eyes. He had a big tube going down his throat and one in his nose; his eyes were really puffy and swollen shut and as chocolate as he was they were still black and blue. It looked as if they were filled with fluid they were so puffed out. I pulled back the sheet covering his body and saw both his damn legs were in casts and elevated. I already knew that when Sophia saw this, she was gon fuckin' clown. I don't know how long I stood there looking at my boy but when I turned around the nurse was still posted up, so I told her I was ready to see my other son, Jonathan.

She led me to the next room and I saw the same shit, except worse. I asked the nurse why they had his head taped down like some damn animal. She said it was to keep his head stable because of the many seizures he'd been having and I'll be damned if his ass didn't have one while I was standing there. I jumped back real quick when his body started shaking all over the place. The nurse ran over to his bed and pressed a button and after a few seconds the shaking stopped. I felt somebody tapping me on my shoulder and turned around to find one of the men who were guarding the door. I turned back around, put my eyes back on my son then leaned down to hear what he had to say. I shook my head up and down then he left. I pulled a chair up to the bed and took a seat. With all three of my boys fighting for their lives all I could think about was whose mama was gon have hell to pay for bringing their bitch ass son into this world.

~SOPHIA~

After Shalom helped me up off the floor, I looked up and saw my assistant minister, his wife and some of the other saints standing next to me. The minister's wife held out her arms and I ran into them like I was a two-year-old little girl and wept. She held me so close and tight I didn't want to let go. Although she was only a few years older than me it felt like the embrace of a mother and child. I cried and wailed for a good twenty minutes. I couldn't help it. I just couldn't help it! Once I pulled myself together I saw Shalom engulfed in the arms of another sister in Christ. I walked over to my only girl, took her hand, then walked over to the nurses' station and asked the ER nurse if we could have some privacy. Without hesitation she led us to a quiet room and closed the door behind her as she exited. The room was small but big enough to fit the two of us along with all the saints who had come to give me support. I know they saw that whole fiasco that was played out in front of them and I know they saw me acting a damn fool but I also knew they understood. If nobody else in the ER waiting room understood, I knew they did and that's all that mattered to me.

With the door closed, the assistant minister asked us all to hold hands while he led us in prayer. I know I should have been up there checking on my boys, but there was no way in hell I was going up there without finding out what had put them there in the first place. I'd been in the streets long enough to know what they have to offer, and the way my baby girl was looking, I didn't want to see my boys without Jesus walking with me and holding my hand. After the prayer I asked if we could sing a few songs because I had to get my mind right. I HAD TO GET MY MIND RIGHT! I already knew that once I saw my sons, my heart was going to be broken. I don't know how I knew, I just did. We sang a few songs and I asked if we could say another prayer. I was so scared to see what awaited me on that third floor, that after the prayer, I sat there numb, and that's when I realized I was more than scared, I was terrified.

This was the first time Shalom had ever been in the presence of my church family. She didn't say a word during any of the praying or singing but I did feel her squeeze my hand real tight throughout the whole ordeal as tears rolled down her face. Once the singing and praying were over, I asked Shalom to tell me everything, from the very beginning that happened that night. When she opened her mouth to speak, the saints all rose up to leave. I guess they didn't think I'd want them all up in my business like that, but that was furthest from the truth. I needed them to hear this story just as much as I needed to hear it for myself, so at my prompting, they sat back down. We turned our attention towards Shalom, waiting for the mystery of the day to unfold.

What my daughter told me would cause a tiny seed bud of hate to be planted into my heart, but it wouldn't be towards the man or men who had done these things to my sons, it would be towards my Joseph.

~SHALOM~

"Mommy, what I'm about to tell you is going to break you down so please be patient with me as I start from the beginning."

~SOPHIA~

My baby took a deep breath, and closed her eyes. Her left leg started shaking so fast, it looked as if she had a severe health condition. With tears streaming down her face, she opened her pretty browns and charted the course that would change my life forever.

~SHALOM~

"Ok, about three years ago I met a man and fell in love. I've kept him away from the family because I already knew Daddy wouldn't approve. You know how Daddy is, Mommy, he's just so controlling and is always going too far and beyond when it comes to me so I didn't tell him, I couldn't. Jude knew about him and tried to warn me, Mommy, he tried to warn me, but I was in love. I also told Jude that he had better not open his mouth about him either. You know me and Jude were two peas in a pod, but even that relationship has been tarnished because of him."

~SOPHIA~

"Shalom, none of that matters now. Please just start from the beginning, baby. Please just start from the beginning."

~SHALOM~

"Alright Mommy, I was coming out of the courthouse and accidentally bumped into Philip. My papers blew all over the place and I was super mad because I had to be back in court within fifteen minutes and didn't have time for no extra nothing. Philip was very apologetic and helped gather my whole damn case, oh! Please forgive me; I'll try to do better with my cursing. But anyway, he helped me gather my whole dang on case before it blew away with the wind. Initially I hadn't looked at him because my mind was on losing vital and confidential information but once I had everything situated, I embraced the hand that was extended to me and then looked up. He was so handsome, Mommy. He reminded me a whole lot of Daddy. Anyway, he tried to make small talk but I was really on a tight schedule and couldn't stay so he walked with me down the street to the cafe I was going to. We were able to converse a little as I grabbed a veggie burger, and then headed back to the building. While en route we introduced ourselves, exchanged contact information then went our separate ways. Although I thought he was fine, I was so swamped in work that our encounter was quickly placed in the 'I might check on this another day' compartment of my life, and I went about my business.

"Three months after our initial meet and greet Philip called. I had forgotten who he was so he had to remind me and when my memory was stimulated, I got excited all over again. We talked on the phone a lot and found we had a few mutual friends. Nobody either of us were particularly close to, just acquaintances. Because I was always swamped at work, it left very little time for play. It would be Philip's patience and understanding that would pull me in and draw me closer into his web of deceit.

"I kept my family a secret for over a year. I knew he may have had an idea of who Daddy and the boys were but I wasn't offering up any info and for the most part he didn't ask for any. But during our second year he started asking me why I hadn't introduced him to you guys. Asking if I was ashamed of him because he wasn't of our caliber. I told him on more than one occasion that my family was not people he wanted to meet because we were cut from a totally different cloth but in time he wasn't trying to hear that either. It would be because of Jonathan's dumb ass. Dang! Ok, I'm sorry. It would be because of Jonathon that he would find out who the people in my family really were.

"It was during Jonathan's trial, and the footage that was shown on TV, that Philip would learn about Daddy. I had refused to introduce him to Jonathan or Jacob because I know how ignorant they could be when it came to certain types of guys. But when he saw me and Jonathan together, walking out of the courthouse, with Daddy trailing close behind, he put two and two together, so I finally told him yes, my dad was the notorious pimp, Joseph. Philip just nodded, then told me he understood why I wanted to keep that tidbit of information on the low-low. When that man said those words, it was like a weight had been lifted off my shoulders and we continued to live our lives as if that vital piece of information had no bearing on our relationship.

"Philip and I couldn't spend a lot of time together because of my hectic work hours, but when were able to squeeze in a moment or two, it was like magic. I knew Philip wasn't caked-up the way I was, so I didn't expect him to take me on exotic vacations or anything like that, but the things he did do made exotic excursions sound like trips to the zoo. One day he took me downtown to the canal. I really didn't think much of it because that's something I could do every day. But on this night Philip had taken a regular old table and chair set, placed them in the center of the garden and had it set for dinner for two, with candles and everything. I thought that shit was romantic as hell! Sorry! But yeah, it was so beautiful and welcoming. As the other couples walked by I could see the women looking at their men like, 'You better be takin' notes, nigga'. That night was perfect. It was so perfect, Mommy. And then on another night, he took me to a place called 'Ours', on the avenue. He said it used to be called 'The Pit' back in the day."

~SOPHIA~

"Where did you say this place was?"

~SHALOM~

"It's on Mass. Ave, close to downtown."

~SOPHIA~

"Ok, continue."

~SHALOM~

"So, we went to Ours which is kinda a hole in the wall jazz joint but the ambience and energy in that room was to die for. I had never been in a place like that. The guys I had previously dated took me to Symphony on the Prairie or Clowes Hall on campus so this was definitely out of my norm. The artiest leaned more towards the New Orleans sound and so did the food. The jambalaya was always on point and so was the gumbo! It was such a cool place it soon became one of our regular spots.

"But our most romantic outing took place at his house. He lives in one of the newly renovated apartments downtown, right around from the jazz joint. He had planned this dinner to perfection. We had been out and about running some errands and when we pulled up to his place he put his finger up to his lips and motioned for me to turn around. He then blindfolded me, got out, ran around to my side of the car, opened the door, and while holding my hand, led me up to his apartment. That was a scary walk. It took a real leap of faith on my part to trust him as he used gentle words instructing me on what to do and when to do it. When we made it upstairs, I didn't realize we were all the way 'up' stairs. Philip slowly removed the blindfold and that's when I noticed that we were on the roof of his apartment. And as before, there was a table set for two but the kicker was that Philip had one of the bands from the jazz club up there waiting on us and as soon as the blindfold came off, they started playing my favorite songs. I could not believe that he had invested so much energy and time for little ole me. That was the best date I'd ever been on.

"You know what, Mommy? A very odd thing happened the first time I went to Philip's place. It was before he'd found out who Daddy and the boys were. Although Philip knew we were swimming in paper, there was no shame in him showing me where he lived. His place wasn't shabby or anything, he just knew I liked the finer things in life and was raised to appreciate those things. As he was showing me around I saw the picture of a very pretty lady on his coffee table, so I picked it up. I turned around and asked him who she was and he said that it was his mom and that she'd died a long time ago. I don't know why I'd asked that question because he was the spitting image of the women in the photo. Then he asked me the strangest thing; he asked me if she looked familiar. I looked at him like he was crazy and asked, 'Why would she?' I put the photo down then continued my personal tour of his crib as I felt him shooting daggers in my back."

~SOPHIA~

For some reason, I got a real sharp pain in the pit of my stomach. I broke out in a cold sweat and thought I was going to pass out. Everybody turned to me and asked if I was ok. One of the sisters had a real concerned look on her face as she started fanning me. I brushed her hand to the side and told Shalom to pay no attention to me and to finish the story.

~SHALOM~

"Ok, Mommy. So, Philip knowing who Daddy was allowed me to set aside my anxiety and invest 100% into our relationship. Well, maybe 95% because Jude finding out about Philip was by pure chance.

"Because I was trying to keep our relationship on the hush-hush, Philip and I had most of our dinner or dates outside the city. I didn't want any busybodies all up in our business and Philip couldn't agree more. It was during one of our dinner outings that fate would have it that Jude and I wound up at the same restaurant and that's where secrets would unfold.

"Jude caught me by surprise when I looked up from my menu and beheld him walking through the restaurant door. Our eyes locked on each other for half a second and they both said, 'You keep my secret, I'll keep yours.' My brother walked past us without so much as a nod and I was grateful for that, but as soon as he was seated we started texting each other back and forth. He started the war of words by texting, 'That nigga's a snake in the grass, shut that shit down.' I text his ass right back and asked, 'How the hell you know?' And it was on from there. I shoulda known something was up. Although I wasn't looking at Philip and at my menu, I could feel him shooting daggers at Jude just as he'd done me.

"The restaurant we were dining at had mirrors everywhere, and since Philip and I were sitting across from each other, I could see that his eyes were averted a little too far to the left which let me know his ass wasn't looking at me nor listening to me. But how could he be listening when his eyes were glued to the mirror behind me, trying to catch every word that dropped outta my brother's mouth.

"Jude and I never talked about that little run in at the restaurant but every chance he got he threw some shade my way about Philip. I knew what my brothers and Daddy did for a living so as far as I was concerned he needed to throw that air in somebody else's direction because I wasn't tryin' to hear it. Philip knew what my father and brothers did for a living as well, and on the sly told me that he too had a couple of corners where he did a little sumthin-sumthin on the side, but that he wasn't tryin' to get rich, just tryin' to maintain. I never asked and he never volunteered any information on what that sumthin-sumthin was, and to be honest I really didn't care. As long Philip and I were able to spend some quality time together that was all that mattered to me. So what he did on the side needed to stay right there, on the side.

"After that situation with Jude died down, I started noticing Philip asking me questions about my family. Nothing outright, just small subtle things like, 'So where's ya mom work' or 'You gotta lotta family here,' questions that at the time didn't carry no weight. I remember Daddy always telling us, 'Don't tell nobody in the streets ya business or ya business will be in the streets,' which led me to tell that nigga the total opposite of what was the truth. I was in love with Philip, but at one time I was also in love with Christian, Nathanael, Thomas, Joshua, Emmanuel and many more so I learned early on to keep my family life and love life on two separate ends of the spectrum. Although I wasn't giving up any info about my personal life, Philip sure in the hell was giving me plenty about his.

"Philip told me he was a 30 year old divorced father of two. He never brought his kids around but he was never shy about showing me pictures of them either. They were his pride and joy. At times he'd ask for a little legal advice because his ex-wife was always diggin' deep into his pockets whenever she felt the threat of another woman coming into his life. Ya know, real insecure moves women make when they know they've messed up. And that's why we bumped into each other on the courthouse steps, because he was reading another outlandish text from her while trying to be on time for an appointment he'd set to fight for his visitation rights.

He said he met his wife when they were both in the Army, stationed in Germany and that it was lust at first sight. After their tour was over they got married and moved here to be close to her family because she was pregnant. He had no problem with that because other than his mom, he really didn't have any other family so he settled down and became a Hoosier. He said after the divorce he felt really lost because he went from seeing his kids every day to seeing them whenever she allowed. Because of that he put on his boxing gloves and started fighting for his rights, a fight that still continues to this day, or so I thought. My throat is starting to get dry, can I get some water?"

~SOPHIA~

"Sure, baby. Brother Cain, could you please bring us all some water? I'm starting to get a little parched myself. I probably don't have any fluids left in me with all these tears I been crying."

As Brother Cain walked out I turned my attention back to Shalom and said, "Go ahead, baby, go ahead and finish telling us the story."

~SHALOM~

"So with my busy schedule and his drama, the time we spent together was a well needed release. But I wasn't for the extra; I got enough of that in the courtroom. My not meeting his kids didn't bother me one bit; besides, I wanted him to myself anyway. Philip has a 9 to 5 as a full time recruiter on the West Side of Indianapolis that allows him a lot of free time to be about the business of seeing his kids. He's well-traveled and basically just keeps to himself. But it wasn't until tonight that I learned that every damn thang that man told me was a lie."

~SOPHIA~

Brother Cain walked in with the water and it couldn't have come at a better time. That cool fluid cascading down my throat was a well needed diversion. As I was drinking my water, I looked at my daughter over the rim of my cup and got that same sick feeling in the pit of my stomach and started throwing up. It's like my body was telling me I didn't want to hear what she has to say but I knew in my mind whether I wanted to hear it or not, I had to.

I was extremely grateful that the trashcan was to my right. With the room being as small as it was, I'm positive I would have gotten everybody covered in my bodily fluid while throwing up. I was surprised at how much came outta me considering I hadn't eaten in hours but when my stomach was on "e" for empty, I kept my head in the trashcan dry heaving. I felt a cold towel being placed on the back of my neck as Brother Cain removed the dirty trashcan, and replaced it with a clean one. A couple of minutes later he placed a bottle of mouthwash and a cup into my hands. I opened that minty fresh liquid, gargled real good, then spit and dumped what remained into the wastebasket. A couple of the other brethren got up, exited, and went to the waiting area so that there'd be enough room for me to lay down on the couch. My eyes were closed as I felt another cool towel being placed on my forehead and the front of my neck. I was sooo grateful for my church family! Lord knows I was so, so grateful! When I opened my eyes, I could see Shalom at the end of the couch, looking at me with fear in her eyes. I gave her a faint smile and told her, "I'm going to be alright, Shalom, with The Lord and God's people, I'm going to be alright."

I must have fallen asleep because when I opened my eyes, there was a whole new set of saints in the room with us and I saw Shalom curled up in a ball in a chair in the corner. Then I looked up and saw Joseph standing in the door looking at me. For some reason I got the feeling he'd been standing there for a very long time. His phone started ringing, he looked at it, sent it to voicemail and said, "Jude's outta surgery," then left.

~JOSEPH~

The nurses said that they didn't have any available beds on the third floor, which meant that Jude would be getting his care somewhere else. I politely told them that they asses had better start playing musical beds up in that bitch because my boys were going to be together. I guess word got around about who I was because the next thing I knew that floor looked like a chess game with my boy being the last play as Jude was being moved into a room next to Jonathan. Checkmate nigga! They better recognize!

I got the rundown about all four of my kids from a group of surgeons who greeted me with outstretched hands and introductions. But before a word could twirl off their tongues I told them to not speak over my damn head and to make that shit as simple as peanut butter and jelly, so they did. They informed me that Jacob had been shot three times, twice in his chest and once in his leg and that he had both legs in casts because a lone bullet had ricocheted off one leg and into the other. They said that Jonathan had been shot three times as well, in his head and both legs, and that of the three, Jonathan was the most stable and should have no problem returning to a normal way of life. When they got to Jude, I couldn't believe my damn ears when they told me that my baby boy had taken most of the bullets. They said that he had been shot seven times and had sustained the most brain and internal damage. When they said that, my damn heart started to bleed, but the world would never see a drop of it. The only blood they'd see would be the blood of the niggas who did this to my boys running down the sewers on the streets of Indianapolis. They let me know that baby girl had minor injuries and had made it a top priority to let the EMT and nursing staff know to not, under any circumstances, cut Jacob's hair. Who in the hell thinks of shit like that at a time like this? But that was my Shalom; always looking out for her boys, if only she'd been looking closer to the one she was fucking, cause that nigga's a dead man walking.

I thanked the surgeons for savings my sons' lives and they asses had the nerve to reply by saying, "We're not out of the woods yet."

I looked at them like, *Y'all's asses gon be in the woods if something happens to one of my muthafuckin' kids.*

They musta got the message because the next set of words that floated out of their mouths was, "Anytime, Mr. Joseph, anytime." *That's what the hell I thought.*

I left my direct number with the hospital staff and the men guarding my boys then went to look for Sophia's ghost ass. It was probably best that she wasn't up there while I was, but damn. I thought she'd at least make her way to the third floor once Jude was outta surgery. Yeah, I couldn't wait to find her negligent ass. When I walked into the ER waiting area she was nowhere to be found. I went to the front desk and they pointed me to the quiet room. I thought *it might be quiet now but I'm bout to ruffle some feathers bout her not going to see our damn sons* but when I opened that door and saw Sophia asleep on that couch, she looked so damn peaceful I left her alone. I knew that as soon as she woke up that that little piece of peace she was experiencing was going to be snatched away.

I don't know how long I stood there looking at Sophia, but I know it was a long time. When my phone rang, it was hard for me to take my eyes off her beauty. And although she had our four kids her body was just as desirable as it had been before she had our first. I looked at my caller ID and knew I had to bounce. It was time for me to go make some mamas some very sad women. I looked up and saw that Sophia was awake and looking at me. I told her, "Jude's outta surgery" then set the wheels in motion for a bloodbath, starting with that traitor, James.

~SOPHIA~

My back was killing me. As I was getting myself together I noticed personal items in the center of the table that were left for our entire group. After gathering some supplies and walking towards the door, I heard everybody stirring behind me. I turned around and gave everyone smiles of gratitude while making my exit, but before I took two steps Shalom was on my heels. I let her know that with or without the complete story, it was time for me to check on my sons. As I was walking towards the bathroom she yelled, "You can't go see them yet, Mommy, Philip works for Daddy!"

I almost sprang my ankle turning around to look at her. I tilted my head to the side and asked, "What the hell did you just say?" I started getting that pain again, but I ignored that mess because nothing was going to stop me from hearing what this child had to say.

My brothers and sisters in Christ were standing behind Shalom with their care packs in their hands, but my eyes got that tunnel vision again, and all I saw was my daughter. I was tired of the drawn out story, it was time for her to get to the point, so that's what she did.

~SHALOM~

"Mommy, everything was a setup. Our meeting, the kids and the life he talked about was all lies. That was the life of his half-sister. He ain't never been in no military and he ain't no recruiter, his ass is a pimp, just like Daddy. He said when he was a little boy after his mother died, Daddy took him under his wing and taught him the tricks of the trade the same way he had Jacob, Jonathan and Jude. He said that the shit that happened tonight was payback. Nobody knew what the hell he was talking about and it seemed he'd hit the pipe one too many times.

~SOPHIA~

I held up my hand and told Shalom to stop. I closed my eyes real tight. So tight they started to hurt. When I opened them the tears came. I asked everyone to go back into the quiet room as I heard Joseph's voice in my head saying,
Public places equal public faces. The world was going to get the scraps of our life from the media, no need in giving them solid information. After we marched back into the quiet room and closed the door I asked everyone to have a seat. Nobody said a word.

Lord knows I did not want to hear what Shalom had to say. I! DID! NOT! WANT! TO! HEAR! IT! Subconsciously I started pullin' out my hair, handfuls of it until a saint came over to me, put both her hands on the sides of my face and quietly said, "Sophia, my sweet Sophia, it's ok, baby. No matter what, it's going to be ok. You are not alone; He is here. He's been here from the very beginning. From the time Joseph opened that door to right now and never forget, we ain't going nowhere, ever!" I know what she was saying was right, but her boys weren't fighting for their lives, she wasn't married to the biggest hustler in town, she didn't have a thousand monkeys on her back trying to pull her in one direction while trying to stay faithful to another. I eventually pulled myself together, and listened.

~SHALOM~

"I am sooo sorry, Mommy. I was so busy trying to keep everybody out of my business, I couldn't see the obvious that was right in front of me and I am so sorry for that! But yeah, everything he told me was a boldface lie.

"You see, Jacob, Jonathan, Jude and I were about to head home from a friend of mines birthday party. When we reached the car we heard somebody yell Jacob's name, so we all turned around and that's when somebody started shooting. Mommy, that shit caught us so fuckin' off guard! I ain't never been in no situation like that before so I started working off adrenaline. We all jumped into the car, bending down trying to dodge the hail of bullets. Jonathan started it, put it in drive and was trying to pull off, but we didn't get far because we ran into a tree. That's when Philip walked his bold ass right up to me and said, 'I guess I'll see ya Daddy at all y'all's funerals and started emptying another round inside the car. That's why Jude got it the worse, because he was trying to protect me, Mommy, he was trying to protect me!"

~SOPHIA~

When Shalom said the word funeral, I thought I was gonna get sick again, but I didn't. I ran over to my daughter and held her tight as she broke down in my arms. One of the deacons asked everyone to form a circle around Shalom. I then listened to one of the most powerful prayers of love, hope and healing that I'd ever heard. I looked up and saw a few of the sisters with tears running down their faces and although I know they may not have been able to comprehend the depth of my pain, I was grateful that they were there to hear the story for themselves because I knew that this was a story I never wanted to speak on again.

Shalom pulled herself together and said that she was ready to finish the story, but little did I know that what she'd show me would seal the fate of my relationship with Joseph, because ain't no way in hell I'd let a dollar nor greed dominate my common sense.

My curiosity was starting to get the best of me, so before Shalom could get started with the remainder of her story, I asked her if she had a picture of this Philip in her phone and she said she did. When my baby placed that phone in front of me I thought I'd seen a damn ghost, because the face looking back at me was none other than that of my rival from my past, Phoebe.

~JOSEPH~

One day, while flicking through channels looking for that nigga, I'd forgotten to hit the damn mute button. I heard one of them pimps tell the audience that the verse that says, "Thou shalt not bow down thyself unto them, nor serve them, for I Jehovah thy God am a jealous God, visiting the iniquity of the fathers upon the children, upon the third and upon the fourth generation of them that hate me." Exodus 20:5, don't apply to us today, and that every man is accountable for his own sins. If I were foolish enough to donate to that TV station, I'd ask for a refund because from my end of this drama, my boys were paying for my sins and a whole lotta other peoples' sins too.

~JACOB~

Why in the hell cain't I open my damn eyes? And what's with all that beeping? Dang this is weird. It's like I'm having one of those dreams where my brain is working but my body is having trouble catching up. Wherever I am, I know my daddy was here, I can smell his cologne. Is that a door opening? And who in the hell is doing all that screaming? Oh, that's mom. What in the hell she screaming for and WHY CAN'T I MOVE! I feel my mama put my hand into hers. I'll never forget the touch of my mom's hands, they're baby bottom soft. Her scent either because no matter the time of day, she always smells fresh, just like now.

What'd she just say? I'm in the hospital because I've been shot? Not just me but my younger brothers too? Ohhhh shit! Now it's coming back to me. The party, the car, somebody calling out my name. Yeah, that was a good one, a real smooth move. I hope that move was a calculated one and them niggas counted the cost. This shit is gon cost them they life because my pops is about to bring murder and mayhem to the streets of Indiana...

~SOPHIA~

It was time for me to face my fears and go see about my sons. I refused to meet the fork in the road alone and asked a couple of the sisters to accompany Shalom and I to the third floor. They agreed and held my hand as I took the longest elevator ride of my life. When we reached our destination the sisters had to persuade me to exit because I couldn't move. I didn't want to move! I slowly left the safety of that metal box and walked down that long dreary hallway with a heartbeat that was so loud, I was sure it could be heard down in the ER. One of the sisters led me to one of my boy's room and as I stood outside that door, I squeezed the hell outta their hands trying to prepare myself for what was to come.

When I walked in and saw my baby laid up in that bed with all those tubes, I automatically bent my knees and was about to hit the floor, but I thank God somebody was there to catch me. *Where's Joseph?* I felt like I was in the Twilight Zone and couldn't move. I don't even know how long I stood in the doorway, but eventually, with my hand over my mouth and tears streaming down my face, I slowly made my legs move in the direction of Jude's bed and although he was just a few feet away, that walk felt like The Green Mile. *Where's Joseph?* The closer I got the worse he looked. *Oh my God, oh my God, oh my God! Oh Lord Jesus please help me! JESUS!*

I stifled my screams while heaving into my hands. *This cannot be my baby! It just can't be.* My eyes beheld a monstrosity. When I finally made it to my son's bedside, I paid no mind to the tubes he had all over the place and slowly laid my head into the crook of his neck, put my arms around his shoulders and wept. One of my sisters brought me a chair to sit in but I couldn't budge if I wanted too. I took in a huge whiff of my baby and when I smelled his scent I knew it was him, otherwise they would have had to do a DNA test because what I saw and what I smelled were two different things. When I rose up and looked at Jude, I again brought my hands to my mouth. *Lord have mercy! Oh my blessed Jesus. Who did this to my son? Who did this to my beautiful baby? WHERE'S JOSEPH?* All four of my kids were beautiful, but Jude held a very special place in my heart because he was the spitting image of the uncle for which he was named, his Uncle Jude. Beautiful blue black skin that never held a pimple, not even as a teenager. Eyes that were so big and brown girls fell in love with them at first sight, along with his deep dimples. And his hair, although just as pretty and wavy as Jacob's, he kept it in a neat, straight, ponytail without a hair ever being out of place. But this! This was not my Jude! This was not my youngest son! His head was puffy and swollen and when I'd leaned down to hold him in my arms it felt as if I felt his head shake like Jell-O. It felt real mushy and although that shaking feeling scared me nothing was going to stop me from holding my baby.

WHERE'S JOSEPH? I NEED JOSEPH! My sisters in Christ were on either side of me, holding me and rocked with me as I moved back and forth while biting on my knuckles and moaning. My stomach was in knots. *WHERE IN THE HELL IS JOSEPH?* I figured I was in shock, but who wouldn't be if their eyes beheld what I was beholding. I just stood there and stared, but in reality, that was all I could do. I took in every single defect of my perfect child and when I say everything, that's exactly want I mean. What the average person didn't see, I did. Like the small scratch that was on the very tip of his nose, or the tiny piece of glass that was still stuck his scalp, or the small piece of black hair that was embedded underneath his nails, which I assumed was Shalom's since he had been shielding her from the onslaught of bullets. I saw it all, but how could I not? This was my baby boy and I was completely lost. What in the hell do you do when your whole world has been turned upside down? I was in a foreign land and didn't have any sense of direction. *WHERE'S JOSEPH?* Yeah, I had seen some off the wall retarded stuff when I was out in them streets, but I'm not in the streets, I'm at home and trouble had finally made its way to my front door, and it was most definitely an unwanted guest.

I heard Shalom breakdown behind me. I'd forgotten that she'd gone to the bathroom and had yet to lay eyes on her big brother. I turned around just as she hit the floor screaming at the top of her lungs. I ran over to my only girl, fell to the floor just as she had, and held her so tight, my embrace would have hurt the average person. My child wailed in my arms yelling gibberish only her and God understood. I rocked her back and forth and had to restrain her on more than one occasion because she was pulling out chunks of her hair. All of a sudden she stopped, then looked at me. She straightened up her face and said *"mommy?"* then got strangest look on it. I didn't even respond, and to be honest, I was scared to speak because the look she had on her face was almost deranged. She said it again, except this time she sang it "mooooommy" then she started crying again. She began rocking back and forth then started beating her fist against her thighs real hard, and then outta nowhere screamed "moooommy, I had a dream last night! Mooooommy! Nooooooo! Moooooommy!" As soon as she said those words I threw up, then passed out.

~JOSEPH~

I know I had to have been sitting in my car for a good two hours after I left my seed up in that hospital. My mind was all over the damn place and I knew I couldn't operate with precision like that, but every time one of my kids' faces popped into my head my damn mind went blank. It was like it was too much information for my brain to handle in one dosage, and because I knew some shit had to be handled, I would have sat in that bitch till kingdom come if I had to. Naw partna, I ain't one to be making no mistakes, so I sat in my car thinking of a master plan. I fired up a joint to calm my mind and smoked that shit while watching those holy rollers make another shift change. I sure hope Sophia didn't think her peeps were going to pray this shit away because tonight, this here is the devil's battle, and ain't no way in hell I'ma let her so-called God or nobody else snatch this moment away from me.

I was blowing smoke out the crack in my window when my phone started ringing. My phone had been blowing up nonstop. I let it ring out and go to voicemail because I knew them walking dead niggas wasn't going nowhere. If they had to die another day then so be it, that shit didn't bother me none. I knew those moving corpses were walking down the road of inevitability, a path that they had paved for themselves, and that the last chapter of their lives had already been written. So hell naw I wasn't in no rush, shit, I been hosting the disappearing show for years and it just so happened that these niggas willingly volunteered to participate in the next act. But my kids, man, I just could not get my kids' faces laying in those hospital beds out of my head, especially my baby boy's face. His shit was damn near twice its normal size. *Damn!* Now, I ain't new to the streets and know this type of hand comes with the card game you playing, but hell, I'm usually the one making bitches widows and kids orphans, not the other way around, but unlike the average street nigga, I gets down for mine and a few played moves is gonna cause some innocent victims to be used as trump cards.

My phone started ringing again; I took another toke off my joint, blew, and then picked it up. It was the hospital calling 911. I sat there, took another pull, blew, stared at my phone and thought *these muthafuckas bet not be calling me bout one of my damn kids.* I smoked that bitch all the way down, turned on some Anita Baker and let her take me down the road of sweet love. As I'm tapping my hands on the steering wheel I see Sophia's MP3 player in the passenger seat. I turned Anita down real low, put one of Sophia's earplugs in my ear, and then pressed play. It took me a minute, but when I recognized the voice, I was blown away. I heard Sophia's ass on there singing Amazing Grace, and that shit was sounding good as fuck. Then I thought, *when the hell she have time to do that? Better yet, whose studio is her ass at?* I skipped a couple of songs and there she was again, singing something about how she don't want the Lord to move some mountain. I didn't know what the hell that was all about, so I skipped up a couple more and got the surprise of my life. I didn't know if the speaking voices were recorded intentionally or not, but I'll be damned if I didn't hear Sophia and The Bitch laughing and giggling and shit. I turned the volume up a lil bit then heard a guy say, *"uh one, two, uh one two three four"* then heard Sophia and The Bitch start singing Precious Lord. I sat back in my seat and looked out into space. All this time I had been thinking Sophia's ass was singing songs she'd uploaded off the Internet, but all the while she was singing songs with The Bitch, and had boldly allowed her voice to be played in my house. That was a helluva move on Sophia's part, and all the more reason why I shoulda stopped that shit on day one because you cain't be nice to bitches without them taking advantage. My phone started ringing again, but this time I answered. It was the hospital informing me that it was urgent that I make my way up there fast. I reached out and pulled my ashtray onto my lap and started shifting shit around looking for a bud. I found one, and then asked whoever was on the phone what the problem was as I fired it up. The caller said that because of confidentiality laws they couldn't divulge any information to me over the phone. I calmly replied, "Well what the hell you call me for then, bitch" and then hung up. I was thinking that I should gone up there and play ghost on they butts to see how the hell they would react because I'm sure everybody had assumed I had left the premises. That shit woulda been like magic, "Shazam bitches, here I am." But that's what they get for "assuming" because they'd just become the first three letters of the word with they dumb asses.

I didn't feel like fucking with stupidity so I sat in my car for another thirty minutes, making sure my high was on point. I eventually made my way to the third floor, walked up to the nurses station and asked what the deal was. I gave her a look that said, "And you had bet not come at me with no bullshit either." She told me that Sophia had passed out while visiting Jude, and was admitted into the hospital because of vomiting and dehydration. Said that they had to give her an IV so she could get some fluids in her and some meds to help her sleep. The words that woman said kinda messed me up because I knew Sophia was gon clown when she got up here, but not like that. She went on to say that

Shalom had to be admitted as well and given some meds for her anxiety and panic attacks. That shit shocked me too because baby girl has always been a fighter, hell, it didn't matter if it was in the courtroom or with her brothers, she made sure she always came out on top, even if it cost her a broken limb. To hear what that nurse was saying about my rock of a daughter hit me pretty close to my heart. This whole incident was literally breaking my family down which was all the more reason to set the streets of this city aflame. I felt my phone vibrating so I zoned out that bitch ass nurse, and pulled it out. I saw I had a text from one of my dawgs that said, *We got 'em.*

I text back, *Keep them dead muthafuckas alive,* then asked the diarrhea of the mouth nurse for the room numbers of Sophia and Shalom.

I went in to see baby girl first. When I walked into her room and up to her bed I thought my little lady looked like a little chocolate sleeping angel. I know I'm a cold hearted nigga, and I ain't raised no punk ass bitches, not even baby girl, but I know her witnessing that madness last night shook her ass up. When the nurse at the front desk told me how hysterical she'd gotten I didn't even trip. But as I looked down at Shalom now I saw a little bit of peace on her pretty round face and thought, *damn she look just like her mama!*

~

I remember the day Sophia brought her home from the hospital and I had walked in on her breast feeding Shalom. I wasn't one for that mother child bonding shit, so I did a 360 up out the bedroom. Sophia called me back just as I was hitting the stairs. While putting on my jacket I walked back in there with a frustrated look on my face and asked Sophia what the hell she wanted. In a real soft whiny voice, she said, "Joseph, you haven't even looked at her," then burst out in tears. Sophia knew that tears didn't move me, so I wasn't fazed by the waterfall, but then she said, "I cain't do this shit no more." I stood there with my hands in my pockets, rocking back and forth on my heels thinking, *she must want me to beat that ass today.* She slowly took her titty out of Shalom's mouth, left her little ass on the bed crying at the top of her lungs, went into the bathroom, shut, and then locked the door. Now, when Sophia had my sons, shit, that was all she wrote. I wasn't no hands on type of daddy, but I knew them little bastards was gon keep my name alive. The thing is though, I didn't have nothing to do with they asses until they could climb up on my knee, and that's the time I started giving them lessons on life. When Shalom was born and that doctor let it be known that Sophia had given birth to a girl, I left that hospital and Sophia and hit the streets. I hadn't seen nor talked to her until she was discharged and at the crib. And even then I didn't pay her ass no attention. I walked over to the bathroom door, tapped lightly and said, "Sophia, you had best ta bring yo black ass out here and get this baby." When she didn't say shit I yelled, "BITCH, GET YO MONKEY ASS OUT HERE RIGHT THE FUCK NOW!" Then started kicking in the door. I didn't have time for Sophia's stupid ass games and had business to take care of. Shalom was still on the bed screaming at the top of her lungs and the more she cried, the angrier I got. "SOPHIA, *kick* OPEN *kick* THIS *kick* MOTHA *kick* FUCKIN' *kick* DOOR *kick* BITCH *kick*!" When that door came off the hinges, I went into that bathroom and grabbed Sophia by her throat. I threw her ass in the tub, held her ass down with one hand,

and then turned on the shower with the other. She was kicking and screaming and scratching and crying and yelling and getting on my damn nerves. I put my finger up to my mouth and very softly said, "Shhhhhhh" and loosened my hand from around her neck. She was still grabbing at my hands and started coughing when I let up a little bit. I calmly looked her in her eyes and told her, "Today is not the day, bitch. Now, you get yo ass cleaned up, go in that bedroom and put yo titty back in that crying ass baby's mouth. I had bet not hear another muthafuckin' whimper come from baby girl and if I do, yo ass is mine. And when I get back, I had bet not see not one water stain on my muthafuckin bedroom carpet either, ya hear?" With her hands still on mine she shook her head up and down so I let her go. I turned the water off and told her, "Now get the fuck up!" then walked out the bathroom.

I walked into the hallway where one of my hoes was standing with a terrified look on her face, and my sons arranged around her feet. The bitch was kinda new and didn't know how I got down but she got a real quick lesson that day. She was taking care of Jacob, Jonathan and Jude until Sophia got better because my sons were real boys and were rambunctious as hell. I walked up to her and asked, "Why you got my sons in this damn hallway?" She was so scared she didn't even speak; she just put them boys on her hips and back like she was mama monkey and took them to their playroom. I stood there looking at that closed door for about five minutes thinking about how I was going to break her little young ass in real good, and then left the crib.

Three hours later young blood was blowing my phone up. When I got around to answering she started talking so loud and fast I yelled, "BITCH, SHUT THE FUCK UP!" then heard her burst out in tears. I rolled my eyes up in my head and thought, *I'm getting tired of these simple ass hoes, they too damn emotional.* I told her ass to start over and that she needed to talk slower than my muthafuckin' dick strokes. She told me that she had to call 911 because Sophia would not come out the bathroom and had left the baby in the bedroom crying, she said, "Mr. Joseph, I know you told me to not go into certain parts of the house, but the baby wouldn't stop crying and when I put my ear up to y'all's bedroom door I didn't hear nobody moving so I got scared. When I tried to open the door it was locked so I picked it and found the baby on the bed and Ms. Sophia in the bathroom on the floor passed out. I didn't know what else to do so I called 911. When the ambulance got there they started asking me all kinds of questions, but I didn't tell them nothing, Mr. Joseph, I swear." I zoned her congested voice out and thought, *well I'll be damned.* I reeled myself back in and told her to call one of my older hoes to come help her with the kids, then moseyed my ass on up to the hospital.

After being told what room Sophia was in, I started walking towards the elevator then stopped. I could have sworn I had just seen The Bitch walking down the hall in the opposite direction. I turned around and watched the ladies form and mannerism as she walked out the exit door. *Naw, that couldn't be, could it?* I shook that off and made my way to Sophia's room. When I walked in Sophia's ass looked damn near dead. Although she was a chocolate black, from a distance her ass looked ashy as hell. When I got to her bed I thought, *well damn!* Sophia's eyes had these huge black rings around them, her lips were dry and cracked, and the reason her ass looked ashy was because she was, and it wasn't because of that shower water either. I wasn't for the hospital shit, and had only entered those facilities for a hot second when three of my kids were born, so I wasn't going to make this visit an exception to the rule, but looking at Sophia's ass in that bed was fucked up. I had to look at her chest to make sure that bitch rose and fell because her ass really looked dead. I'd had enough of that action and turned to leave. Just as I was reaching to open the door a doctor was opening it and walked in. He introduced himself, then asked if I was Sophia's husband, to which I answered "hell naw!" He asked me my relation, to which I replied, "none" as I again reached for the door. Doc McBrains then asked who they were to contact in case of an emergency. I turned around, looked that stupid genius in his eyes and said, "If she's already in the hospital then there should be no emergencies," then bounced.

When I got to the crib all hell had broken loose. The kids were running all over the place taking all kinds of advantage and I could tell a couple of them needed their diapers changed because the whole house smelled like the sewer. I found young blood in the kitchen getting Sophia's frozen breast milk out the freezer for Shalom. I watched as she put the milk in a bottle, and then the microwave. She looked up and saw me standing there watching her every move, jumped, put her hand over her heart then said, "Whew, Mr. Joseph, you scared the living daylight outta me." When I didn't respond she asked, "Is Ms. Sophia ok?" I just stood there with my hands in my pockets playing with my loose change, and then she said, "Well, nobody ever came to help me so I guess they all workin'." Shalom was in her baby seat and started crying. Youngblood took her bottle out the microwave, and then got a real scared look on her face as she looked down at Shalom while shaking her baby bottle unnecessarily fast, mixing up the milk. Youngblood looked up at me and said, "Shit, Mr. Joseph! I gotta run out to my car right quick to get a pad, I ain't had no time to change it with the baby and the boys, I'll be right back." She ran in my direction and handed me Shalom's bottle. She took the stairs by twos, ran back downstairs then slammed my damn front door as she ran out my house and I'll be damned if I didn't hear her little hooptie start up and then pull off. I ran to that door so fast I had to jump over a couple of my kids. I swung my front door opened and thought, *now I know her little scrawny ass did not just leave me with all these got damned babies.* As soon as I had that thought Shalom's ass started hollering. I was like Flo Evans from Good Times: "DAAAMN! DAAAMN! DAAAMN!"

It was like my boys knew I had been setup and got a kick out of my predicament because they little asses started running in and out between my legs and made me almost bust my ass. I picked up the phone line real quick, trying to get in touch with one of my other hoes, but I guess Youngblood was right, all them bitches was workin' and not answering their phones nor my pages. *Shit!* Sophia's ass was gon pay for this!

I walked over to baby girl and looked down at her as she was hollering and squirming around in her chair turning all red and shit. The boys were running and screaming they damn selves until I yelled, "Y'all better shut the fuck up!" They little asses froze like statues, which caused me to start cracking up. Shalom was still crying as I told my little soldiers that I needed their help. I didn't know a damn thang about no babies and since they asses were always up under they mama I had to use the resources that were available to me. My little troops made me proud as I watched Jacob take the bottle from me and place a little drop on the back of his hand. That shit made him break out into tears. Young blood had placed a cloth baby diaper around the bottle which sucked up all the heat so when little man started crying, I snatched that shit outta his hand and did what I saw him do. Well I'll be damned, that bitch was tryin to kill my damn baby cause that shit was hot as hell. I took out my phone trying real hard to get ahold of one of my bitches but they asses was still on they back. *Damn!* I had to get this shit under control. I ran upstairs, got a cool face towel and put it in Jacob's little wrist. I had seen Sophia give them popsicles and sit them in front of the TV when they got on her nerves so I ran to the freezer, opened it up, then froze my damn self.

How in the hell was anybody gon find anything in this bitch with it being packed to capacity? I had to take half that shit out before I hit gold. I took out twelve of them damn thangs, told my boys to follow me into my all white den, and then started poppin' those sickles open. I had my back to my boys and didn't think they'd followed me because they were real quiet. I turned around and all three were still standing in the hallway. They knew that the den was the "no-no" room and feared crossing the threshold. I put those cold sticks down, walked over to my troops, and got down to their level. A couple of the asses stank real bad but I would hafta deal with shitty asses later, I had more pressing matters to deal with. I looked them all eye to eye and said, "Now boys, y'all know this is Daddy's room, right?" They all shook they heads up and down, "and you know I'll beat ya little ass if you come up in here, right?" Again, they shook they little snot nosed heads up and down. "Well today is a special day because you got a new little sister, so, because of her y'all get to come I'm my special room, cool?" They got big cheesy smiles on they faces then made a mad dash for my $12,000 Italian leather couch. My insides cringed as they started jumping on my shit. I said, "Fuck it," gave the remote to Jacob, gave them four sickles a piece, then ran to see about baby girl who was screaming like she was about to die. Yeah Sophia, you gon pay for this shit!

Amongst all the crap I had placed on the counter, I saw some more of Sophia's breast milk. I called Jacob back in into the kitchen because I didn't know what to do. I watched as he took the little plastic container, put it in a bottle then held up three fingers then five. I didn't know what the hell that meant until I remembered that hot ass bottle that bitch had made. I snatched the bottle out of his hand and ran to the microwave. Shit, I was happy as hell I knew how to work that bitch. I put the bottle in for thirty five seconds and turned around to see Jacob with his popsicle hanging out of his mouth and snot running down his nose, trying to unfasten Shalom's safety belt. I gave little man a kiss on the top of his head and told him that I think I could take it from there. I watched as he skipped away from me, and then disappeared around the corner. I stood up with my hands on my waist looking down at that little squirmy crying thing. The microwave beeped, I took the bottle out and again, did what I saw Jacob do, and put a little drop on the back of my hand, perfect! I stared at that little drop for a hot second and thought, *I wonder what this shit taste like* then licked the back of my hand. *Awww hell naw!* That shit was for the birds! I walked over to baby girl while wiping Sophia's breast milk off my tongue with the wrist of my shirt. I again stood over Shalom and watched her throw a hissy fit over that nasty shit. I picked her baby chair up and placed it on the island. Because my hands were so damn big it took me a minute to get the safety belt unfastened, but when I did, I was still at a loss. How in the world was I going to get that little bitty person in my big ass arms. I didn't know what the hell to do so I took the seat into the living room, gently placed it on the couch, then in super slow motion touched my baby girl for the very first time. I figured if I dropped her or something stupid like that, at least she'd land on something soft. I placed her into the crook of my arm the way I had seen Sophia do with our boys, put the bottle in little Shalom's mouth, watched as she sucked the breaks off that damn thang, and fell in love.

One of my hoes finally made it to the house, but by then I had the crib on lock. The boys had been given baths and in bed while me and Shalom were in the living room, flicking through channels, with the volume on mute, looking for that nigga. I got up and told her to clean up my den because the boys had demolished it. As she was turning to leave she told me that she had gone to see Sophia at the hospital. I gave her ass a cold stare and asked her who gave her permission to do that shit, especially since I had needed her here. She started stuttering out a lie so I told her to shut up and that she had better be grateful my baby was cradled in my arms because otherwise her ass would be on the floor. She then told me that the doctors said that Sophia was suffering from postpartum depression, a condition some women get after having kids, but that Sophia's was a very extreme case. I didn't know what the hell she was talkin' about and really didn't give a damn; I just needed her ass home to be about home business. I dismissed the hoe by turning my attention back to the TV, spread back out on the couch, kissed Shalom on the top of her pretty little head, and then continued flicking through channels, with the volume on mute, looking for that nigga.

~

I looked down at my baby girl in her hospital bed, bent down and gave her a soft kiss on her forehead. I put my lips next to baby girl's ear then whispered, "Them niggas gon pay for this, Shalom, they gon pay for doing this to you, yo brothers and yo mama. I promise you that. Sleep well baby girl, sleep well." I kissed her on her forehead again, and then went to see about Sophia.

I walked into Sophia's room and found her awake. She was looking at the ceiling with tears rolling down the sides of her face. She must not have seen nor heard me because I had been standing next to her bed for a few minutes, and when I had reached out to wipe a tear off the side of her cheek she jumped. I pulled a chair up to her bed, let down the bed rail and held her as she broke down in my arms. Her moans were moans of anguish and despair. All she kept crying was, "Joseph, my babies, my babies Joseph, my blessed, blessed babies, Joseph." That shit broke my damn heart because in spite of our relationship, Sophia loved and cherished our kids. She made sure our family didn't want for shit, and on more than one occasion she accepted a couple of black eyes for her little hearts, blows she willing took because she chose to choose them, over me.

~

I ran my crib like Ft. Knox. When I wanted it quiet, it had best be quiet. Whatever I wanted to eat had better be hot and ready when my elbows hit my dinner table. The kids wore my name when out in them streets. I didn't care if they were in school, the supermarket, the mall, hell, I didn't give a damn if they were in a public bathroom taking a shit. They had better be doing it with dignity, because if they didn't, they'd have hell to pay. One day the whole damn crib was acting suspect. I heard more than the normal amount of whispering and everybody got hella quiet whenever I walked into the room. I acted like all was good but took note of everyone's behavior change. I went to my den, started flicking through channels, with the volume on mute, looking for that nigga when I heard a loud ass slap followed by heated mumbling. I didn't move, just continued looking for that nigga.

That night, while we were alone in the kitchen, Sophia was on edge and jumped at every thump or bump the kids made while getting ready for bed. She was doing the dishes while I was sitting at the bar eating some fruit looking at the "First 48," criticizing how young and dumb today's killers were. When I knew the kids were out for the count, although she hadn't finished doing the dishes, I told Sophia that it was time for bed. She stood at the sink a second too long so I hit the bar and yelled, "SOPHIA!" which caused her to jump, throw down the dish towel then speed walk toward the stairs. Before her foot hit the first step I said, "Sophia, I want black tonight." About five minutes later I heard the bath water being turned on and finished watching my show. In actuality, the show was watching me, because my mind was on what I was going to do to Sophia's ass when I made it up those stairs. I know Sophia knew that no matter how hard her and them damn kids tried to keep shit from me, I always found out, it was just a matter of if she was going to tell me about it or not.

I walked into the bedroom and saw Sophia putting on my favorite perfume. Our eyes connected through the mirror, so to fuck with her I blew her scared ass a kiss, started laughing then went to take my bath. After I eased into the tub, I fired up the joint Sophia had laid out for me, took a sip of my premixed drink, picked up the remote, then started flicking through channels, with the volume on mute, looking for that nigga. As I flicked my mind went into a million different places anticipating my after bath rendezvous. Sophia was getting outta place and it was time for her to be put back in. I had over 50 bitches I had to keep in check, my bitch at home shouldn't be one of 'em.

The water was starting to get cold so I got out, dried off, put on my robe and made my way to the bedroom. As soon as I entered Sophia asked, "Are you ready, Joseph?" In answer to her question, I let my robe drop to the floor; lay across my bed butt naked, flat on my belly, then closed my eyes and thought, *yeah, she's well overdue for this beat down.* Sophia lit the candles, poured the wine, turned off the lights then hit play on the surround sound. The smooth jazz danced into my ears and caused my mind and shoulders to relax. I could hear Sophia pouring the scented hot oil into her hand, then felt her straddle my back. I waited as she vigorously rubbed her hands together then felt her place them on my hot flesh. She started to slowly rub the oil into my back but stopped when I up held up hand. "I suggest you get them shakes under control, Sophia." I put my hand down and waited. With my eyes closed and my anger rising, I heard Sophia drink not only her glass of wine but mine too. I didn't give a damn, I just knew that the next time I felt her touch it had better be a steady one. She squeeze more oil into her hands and rub them together, her palms hit my back stiff as a board, just the way I liked them, and then she started. "Joseph, do you like this, Joseph? Do you like my touch? Huh, baby?" I felt a wet tear hit my back. "Do you, Joseph?"

I held my hand up again which caused her to jump. In a calm soothing tone I said, "Sophia, I ain't got all muthafuckin' night to be dealing with yo ass, now wipe that damn snot off yo face and I don't care if you gotta drink the whole damn bottle of that wine. If I feel them shaking ass hands on my back again I'ma force them bitches down yo throat. Now, go get me another drink and joint cause you dun fucked up my high and gon in there and get yo self together, ok baby." I flipped onto my back before she could move or answer. I looked into her horrified eyes and felt no sympathy for her dirty ass. I told her to give me a kiss, and with tears streaming down her face she bent down and placed her trembling lips on top of mine. With our lips locked I said, "Open them damn eyes, Sophia." When she did I kissed her softly on her left cheek then whispered, "You know I love you don't you?" She started moaning, so I kissed her softly on her right one and then said, "I'm serious, Sophia, I've always loved you. I saw you at that bus station and my damn heart skipped a beat." I started kissing her passionately, rocking her hips back and forth on my dick because I was hard as hell. She laid her head on my chest and started shaking. I slapped her hard on her ass then said, "Sophia, baby, shit! Girl, I love yo muthafuckin' ass." I rolled her onto her back, which gave me the upper hand and then stretched her legs wide. She put her hands over her face and started weeping. I slowly put my dick inside her and although she was terrified, her shit was wetter than Niagara Falls. "Shit, Sophia!" I started stroking that ass while licking her breasts and neck, which caused her ass to cry and moan at the same time. I began to drown in her pool of love, a pool that never quenched my thirst.

With a shaky voice she cried, "I'm sorry, Joseph, please, I'm sorry." I slapped my hand over her mouth and stopped all movement, reached over and turned on the light, then dived back in. I grunted as I slid in and basked in the feel, taste and scent of Sophia thinking I was about to lose my mind because her shit felt so good. I repeated, "Open yo muthafuckin' eyes, Sophia. If I hafta repeat myself I'ma beat yo sneaky ass into tomorrow!" She started crying harder but opened them bitches. That was the last time I had to tell her that. While fucking her ass I said, "Sophia, I don't know why you think you can keep shit from me. Damn yo shit's good!" I stopped for a minute because the more I fucked the angrier I got. I reached over into the nightstand drawer and pulled out my pocket knife. I placed her legs on either side of me then slowly opened that bitch up and started cutting off the sexy ass negligee she'd put on. I then sat back and admired her beautiful body. My mouth started watering as I used the knife to play with her pretty full breasts, and with her eyes on me I bent down and gave both her breasts some tongue action. I watched as her eyes blinked in slow motion as if the ecstasy she was feeling was too much to bear.

I already knew I was going to have to teach Sophia a lesson, it was just a matter of now or later. I threw the knife aside and then listened as her body played me a song. I looked in her eyes and through clenched teeth said, "You know you cain't keep shit from me, right?" While crying, she shook her head up and down. I put my hands on her breasts and gently twirled my fingertips around her nipples. "Why do you make me do this to you, girl? Huh? Aww, shit you feel good." I moved my hands to her shoulders, which caused her to break down. "Now who's going to take that trifling trick ass bitch to get an abortion? Huh? And which one of our boys didn't wrap they shit up? Huh? Huh, Sophia?"

Sophia started saying, "Joseph, it was Jacob, I was going to" but before she could finish with her lie, I stopped fucking, closed my eyes and put my finger to my lips which caused her to shut her mouth like a mouse trap. I started going in and out again, then placed my hands around her neck and said, "You had all damn day to tell me, Sophia! All muthafuckin' day!" I started to squeeze while still going in and out. "Sophia! This is the third time you put them kids before me, hiding shit." As Sophia put her hands on top of mine, I squeezed tighter. "Don't put them before me no more, Sophia." I squeezed a little more and her eyes got bigger and I was still fuckin' her ass. "Are you going to do this again, Sophia? You gon stop hiding shit from me, trying to protect them stupid ass kids? Huh?" Her ass had the nerve to frown, like I had asked her the wrong muthafuckin' question.

I could feel Sophia's legs moving under my weight, trying to lift me up off of her. I took my hands from around her neck, grabbed her face and kissed the hell outta her swollen lips, with our eyes still opened. As I continued going in and out I took my left hand and put both of hers in a vice grip, then took my right one and started playing with her breasts, which were soft as cotton. While stroking her shit, I took that same hand and moved it to her throat. I looked her straight in her eyes and said, "Sophia, I'ma ask you one more time. Are you going to put those muthafuckin' kids before me again?" While still going in and out, I squeezed tighter. Sophia put her hands on top of mine, I squeezed tighter, pushed down on her neck and yelled, "HUH?!" She squealed, yanked hard on my hand, which loosened my grip long enough for her to take in a good deep breath, snort, choke then spit in my damn face. I slapped her ass so hard I thought I broke her neck. While still going in and out I put both my hands around her throat as she fought, squirmed and pulled at my hands. I was in a rage as I tried to squeeze the fuck outta her throat. I saw a tear roll out her left eye as she passed out, and at the same damn time I had the best orgasm of my life, and then passed out on top of her.

From that day forward I asked Sophia absolutely nothing about our kids because I knew her crazy ass, without hesitation, would put her life on the line for them bitches and would shelter them from all hurt, harm or danger, even from me.

~

The nurse came in and gave Sophia something to calm her nerves. I held her hand as she lay back down with a long lost look on her face. I scooted close to her bed, put my mouth close to her ear and in a soft voice told her, "Sophia, I'm going to take care of this baby, ok. I'm going to fix this, ok Sophia?"

She turned her head in my direction and said, "How are you going to make this right, Joseph? Huh? How Joseph, by shedding more blood? Is that your solution? Can't you see that your way doesn't work and that it never has? Why can't you see that?" Her ass started getting loud as hell. I attributed her side talk to them drugs she was taking because she had to be out her got damned mind to be coming at me talking crazy about mines.

I stood up, dropped her damn hand, looked down at her and said, "Sophia, I'ma gon and chalk those words you just spoke to me up to them meds. Now, I'm about to go visit our sons and baby girl, then go handle our family matters." Sophia opened her mouth to respond but before she could I bent down, gave her a kiss, then broke camp.

I made my way to Jonathan's room. When I walked in I was shocked to find that he wasn't in there. My mind went blank as it took me to unfamiliar terrain. I walked out of his room, grabbed the first staff person I saw, and demanded to know where my boy was. The staff member happened to be a maintenance man who looked at me like I was insane. I was about to grab that fool by his throat because I didn't care who he was I was gon shake information out of him until I got what I wanted, even if it was a lie. Outta nowhere a hand touched my shoulder and as I turned around I balled up my big black fist because I was about to pounce on whoever it was, but then I peeped that it was one of the guards protecting my family. He held his hands up and said, "Whoa, whoa partna, they took him to CAT scan so that they could take another look at his brain." Just as he was finishing his sentence, the staff, along with his bodyguard, were wheeling Jonathan back to his room. I watched in amazement as they maneuvered all that shit connected to him without error. I looked down at his arm as they wheeled him past me and saw all them damn needles taped to his wrist and stepped back. Seeing that shit made my own damn arm start to tingle. His nurse told me that it would take a few minutes to get him settled and everything reconnected. I used that as an opportunity to text my henchmen and ask about my prey.

How are my packages?

Two seconds later I got a reply that said, *Bleedin',* so I text back, *let's keep it that way.*

I wasn't no cat and knew I didn't have no nine lives. I'd came to the conclusion that however long it was going to take for me to see every single one of my kids, that was just the time it was going to take. If it took two hours to fulfill my task, then so be it and if it took two weeks, I was still gon be right there until all that I had set out to do was complete. I didn't know what tomorrow held for me so I wasn't takin' no chances. The nurses, along with those hypocrites, came out of Jonathan's room so I went in. How the hell they got gold card access to my family kinda fucked me up but I was going to have to address that at another time.

At Jonathan's bedside I got a little hot and wanted to check the staff about his head still being tied down but left it alone, especially after watching him have that seizure earlier in the day. But that shit really made my boy look like a restrained animal and made me feel some kinda way. Since I wasn't no doctor I said, "Fuck it," pulled up a chair and took a seat. I stretched out my legs, crossed my ankles, and then leaned back trying to get comfortable because that chair was hard as hell. I laid my head back and closed my eyes. Before I knew it I was starting to nod. I allowed my body to consume the rest it needed while my dreams took me down memory lane.

~

Although I was an uneducated nigga, I was smart as hell. I was like the rain man; if 513 toothpicks were falling to the floor I could count them bitches before they hit it. And that's how my Jonathan was, except smarter. Of all my kids, Jonathan was most like me and very rarely let shit get past him. And although I had set the course for my sons' lives by training them in the art of pimpin', Jonathan went to college by day and did his pimpin' shit at night. He paid for his own classes and had the nerve to live on campus, as if he didn't have a 5,000 square foot crib of his own. He was an eye catcher too, just like his daddy. Over six feet tall with a slim, but cocky build. Cold black wavy hair and a keen, sharp Abraham Lincoln nose. His eyes were almond shaped which caused me to look at Sophia sideways when he came out, but as soon as he moved his hungry ass mouth, looking for some food, I saw his dimples and knew he was mine. And although he was just as ruthless and cutthroat as his old man, his little ass had the nerve to be the most spiritual. I don't know where Jonathan got this awakening but it seemed like even at a young age he knew God existed. And although I was anti everything when it came to religious shit, that little boy of mine brought some shit to the table that made the hair on the back of my neck stand up.

In the city of Indianapolis we've been known to have all four seasons in one day. We can have fall in the morning, spring at mid-morning, summer in the afternoon with snow in the evening. Because Mother Nature was constantly on her period, fucking up a nigga's day, Jonathan was always sick, even as a newborn. I made Sophia's ass sleep with him downstairs because his butt cried nonstop and I wasn't tryin to hear that noise up in my castle. At two Jonathan started getting earaches and sore throats. Sophia kept takin' him to the doctor and they kept giving him antibiotics, which suppressed the symptoms but didn't take care of the problem. At three Sophia noticed his speech was funny and that she always had to repeat herself when talking to him. I recall Sophia getting the kids ready for a birthday party and Jonathan running into our room saying, "Meme, dere my tittie sirt?" I was all proud and shit thinkin' *that's my boy, his ass gon be a breast man.*

Until Sophia said, "It's folded up on your bed, you have to look for it, Jonathan." He ran his little ass outta our room before I could pop his little butt for stepping over the threshold.

After he left Sophia noticed the confused look on my face and said, "He was asking about his t-shirt, get ya mind out the gutter." I thought, *how the hell she know that?* I just grunted, sat on the edge of the bed, picked up the remote and started flicking through channels, with the volume on mute, looking for that nigga.

After spending a whole lotta damn money on bullshit doctors, at the age of four we found out that Jonathan needed his tonsils out and tubes in his ears to pop them bitches opened. The day before the surgery, I was soaking in the tub, sipping on my drink, when Sophia tapped lightly on the door. I told her she could come in and when she did she sat on the toilet. I could tell she was nervous and wondered, *what the hell she want now?* I ain't the most patient man so I kept my eyes on the TV and flicked through channels, with the volume on mute looking for that nigga. I took a deep, exasperated breath and said, "Spill it, Sophia, I ain't got all damn day."

She nervously said, "Joseph, I know you don't like hospitals but could you please."

I didn't even let her finish, I said, "Nope" then hit the unmute button to let her know she was dismissed. As soon as she lifted her butt off the toilet to exit, Jonathan's hardheaded ass came flying into the bathroom running his mouth. Sophia was trying to shoo him out but he dodged all her attempts, which made me laugh. Although he was running and talkin' gibberish, all at the same time, I did understand "preeeese dadee." I got a little frustrated and told his little ass to stop running so I could hear what the hell he was sayin'. He stopped so fast he almost toppled over into the tub. I hit the mute button then listened as he started talkin' which made me more frustrated because I didn't understand a damn thing he was saying. I looked up at Sophia with a frown on my face and said, *Interpret that shit.*

She was nervously ringing her hands then said, "He asked if you would go to the doctors with him tomorrow."

I looked at her like, *You put him up to this shit didn't you?* Jonathan came over and put his little curly head on my arm then started speaking in what sounded like a foreign language so I looked up at Sophia like, *interpret, bitch.*

She started talking fast again. "He said that I was supposed to ask you and that I was taking too long."

I gave her a look that said, *He just saved you from a ass whoopin'.* I then looked down at my little man, kissed him on the top of his head and asked, "You gon be a trooper?" He shook his head up and down with a big ass smile on his face. I rubbed his curly top and said, "Alright little man, I'ma be there." He started jumping up and down and twirling and shit. I said, "Come here, Jonathan." He walked over all happy until I asked, "Who gave you permission to come into my room?" I then commenced to beat his little hardheaded ass.

On the day of his surgery I dropped Jonathan and Sophia off at the front door then went to park. Ten minutes later Sophia called me in a panic, asking where I was because they were about to take Jonathan back and he was having a fit because I hadn't made it in. I hightailed it in there and walked into his room just as they were putting the IV in his arm, the very part I was trying to miss. I told Sophia, "I'll be back" as Jonathan burst into tears.

Sophia had been walking towards me but rushed to his bedside like I wasn't even there. Since the whole IV deed was done I stood in the doorway and watched as Sophia softly calmed him down. I heard her ask, "You better now, my little Jonathan? Are you scared?"

Jonathan looked over in my direction but past me, over my left shoulder, and said, "Dot do dore, cuz deedus is dandin hind dadee." For some strange reason I understood every damn word that floated out his mouth. I jumped forward so fast my damn heart skipped a beat, as if somebody had really been standing behind me. I looked at the spot where I once stood and saw absolutely nothing. As I made my way over to Jonathan's bed I put my eyes on Jonathan and he was still staring at the same spot. I kept looking from Jonathan to the spot, Jonathan to the spot. The look I saw on my son's face let me know that if I was to ask his ass the same question, of who he was looking at, in a thousand different ways, his answer would always be the same, Jesus.

About a year later Sophia bought the kids a huge treehouse with her extra coins. She had realized that the inside of a home was not the place for three stair step boys and a newborn baby. She found and bought anything she could to keep them occupied but the more she bought, the faster they lost interest, except for when it came to that treehouse. Sophia hit gold when she made that move because those boys would be out there for hours playing pirate and castle shit, with Sophia having to force them to come into the house so that they could get cleaned up to eat. Their little brains took them to faraway lands and they never wanted to come back, not even for brain juice. If time permitted I would sit out on the back deck, with a remote in my hand, with the volume on mute, looking for that nigga, while they played. Yeah, I had a TV on my deck. My money, my shit. And on the real, I had TVs in every damn room in my house because if the feeling moved me and I wanted to look for that nigga, my ass had easy access. Now, every few minutes I would shift my gaze from the TV and sneak a peek at my boys, then continue looking for that nigga.

One evening, as the sun was starting to set, I turned off my TV, stood up to stretch, then looked into the doorway of the treehouse. Jonathan's eyes met mine as his little five year old ass jumped out the treehouse like he was superman or some shit and landed on his damn head. I moved so fast you'd have thought I was chasing a dollar. By the time I got to him his little raggedy ass was hopping up and running towards the ladder for round two. I stopped dead in my tracks because ain't no way he shoulda got up off that ground alive. I called for Sophia over my shoulder, and when she didn't answer I yelled, "Jonathan, come here!" He climbed back down the ladder and started skipping towards me, I held up my hand and in a stern voice said, "Stop, and keep yo little ass right there till yo mama come." I turned around and stormed into the house yelling, "Sophia, where yo ass at?"

I heard her whisper, "I'm right here, Joseph." She was standing at the kitchen sink, looking out the window, frozen.

I was in such a rush to figure out what had just happened, that I had walked right past her. I asked, "Did you just see that?" She couldn't even speak, she just nodded. She turned around and looked at me and that's when I saw her tears. I shifted my eyes to the backyard and Jonathan was still standing there looking dead at me. I turned back to Sophia and said, "Go take care of that shit." I fixed myself a vodka straight, went into my den, picked up the remote and with the volume on mute, started looking for that nigga.

Later that night, after Sophia had put the boys and Shalom to bed, I had been flicking through channels when I asked her what she thought that shit with Jonathan was about. She said, "I don't know, Joseph. That boy should have been dead." I sat there looking at her dumb ass like, *Tell me something I don't already know, bitch."*

But then she said, "Jonathan said the strangest thing as I was getting him out of the tub, he said he wasn't scared to jump because he knew Jesus would catch him." When she said that, a damn chill went down my spine. We looked at each other in silence for a complete minute. Sophia opened her mouth and was about to say something else but I wasn't trying to hear no more of that weird shit, so I turned my attention back to my TV, un-muted the hypocrites to zone her ass out, and then started flicking through channels, looking for that nigga.

About six months later some shit happened that was so fucked up, I told Sophia to take Jonathan's ass to a psychiatrist cause his ass had to be crazy. I was down with some type of damn flu and was sick as a dog. Sophia had been at my beck and call making sure I didn't want for nothin' and made sure the kids steered clear so they wouldn't catch what I had. My shit had gotten so bad I had Sophia call my private doctor to do a damn home visit cause there wasn't no way I could get out of the bed. The kids knew not to come up in our bedroom, ever, but Jonathan's hardheaded ass made his own rules, especially when he knew his daddy was down.

Jonathan walked his little bold butt into our bedroom like he pay the mortgage. I tried calling for Sophia to come snatch his little ass up, but every time I took in a deep breath I would go into a coughing fit which would cause my lungs to burst into flames. I knew she couldn't hear me because she was downstairs whipping up a recipe some woman had given her that was supposed to break the shit up. So instead of using my energy for a lost cause, I laid there hating the fact that I couldn't put my belt on his little disobedient ass.

Jonathan was at the foot of our bed playing with his toy car having a whole damn conversation with himself. All I could do was listen because I sure in the hell couldn't move. Then he stood up, looked at me then said, "Say hi to Jesus, Daddy, He's standing right next to yoooou, verooooom, beep." He started running around the bedroom waving his arm up and down as if it the air was his invisible racetrack.

All I could do was follow his movements with my eyes because my whole damn body hurt. I whispered, "Come here, Jonathan."

He spun his little ass in circles over to my bed and then climbed aboard. He gently walked on his hands and knees to where I was, placed his head on my chest, yawned then said, "He told me to tell you that He loves you."

Just as Sophia was walking in with my food tray, I looked down at his little head and in a hoarse voice I said, "Who?"

Jonathan yawned again, then whispered, "Jesus", and fell asleep.

I looked up and with what little energy I had left and whispered, "Get this muthafucka up outta my damn bed."

After I told Sophia everything that went down, and what Jonathan had said, we argued for days about whether he should see a doctor or not. I was still laid up but I guess that home remedy had worked because I was feeling better. During our last and final argument, I hit the nightstand with my fist so hard the lamp fell to the floor. I pointed my long black finger at Sophia and through clenched teeth said, "If you don't take my muthafuckin' son to a doctor to see what the hell is going on with his psycho ass, I'ma beat you so bad, you gon wish you were born with no legs or arms cause I'ma break all them bitches."

The next day Jonathan had his first psych appointment. Sophia took his little ass to that doctor for six damn months, all for nothing. Sophia told the doctor all the things that had occurred which prompted us to make the call in the first place. With all the vital information laid out, the doctor used different age appropriate tactics of communication and role playing. Some that included Sophia, to pull what was in Jonathan out, but instead of achieving success, Jonathan's little ass made us look like the crazy ones because he acted like he didn't know what the hell we were talking about.

Sophia told me that whenever it seemed as if Jonathan was about to spill the beans, mid-sentence, he'd stop talking, as if he had immediate amnesia, if there is such a thing. Eventually I told Sophia to stop wasting my money on that quack ass doctor, and that if Jonathan's ass was crazy then so be it. Needless to say, after that last ghost sighting, as far as I know, Jonathan never mentioned Jesus again. Not in my presence anyway.

~

While asleep I heard a tap, tap, tap noise that caused me to open my eyes. I moved and wanted to cuss out the walls because my back hurt so bad. *Damn!* When I was finally able to sit up I looked at Jonathan and saw that his eyes were opened. I got up and walked to my son's bedside. Because his head was still tied down, he couldn't move it, so when he saw movement out of his peripherals he shifted his eyes towards me. I looked down at my boy and thought, *all three of my sons are paralyzed to their bed. Shit, they should be out doin' what young fine boys do. Them niggas gon suffer for this shit.* I heard Jonathan's door open behind me but didn't turn around, I then felt an arm go around my waist. I looked down and saw that it was Sophia. I guess her meds had worn off and she had demanded to be wheeled to one of her kid's rooms. When she learned that I was in Jonathan's she had them wheel her there, IV pole and all. No words were spoken as we stood there looking at our son. None were needed.

Jonathan could feel the love that surrounded him and let out a damn weak ass tear. I put my hand up to my neck like, *Cut that the fuck out.* I know the whole scene was emotional and shit but damn. Amos' men don't function like that, that's what bitches do. But instead of stopping, he cried more. I soon came to realize that his ass knew something I didn't, because before that night was over, the destiny of my entire family would be changed forever.

Sophia was in her wheelchair on my left, and because she was so low, it was hard for Jonathan to see her, but he did the best he could with what he was working with, and was able to see me just fine. Out of the blue, Sophia started singing one of her church songs, which brought to memory that mp3 shit. My ass was so drained I didn't even feel like thinking about it. I watched as Jonathan's eyes went from me to his mother and vice versa, but then his eyes shifted to something or someone over my right shoulder, which caused me to turn around real quick to see who was there. For some reason, deep down, I knew I wouldn't see nobody. I resigned myself to accept what was and said, "Fuck it," because I was too damn drained to be tryin to find invisible niggas. Instead of fighting the funk, I pulled my chair up next to Sophia, sat next to my son's bed and listened as she sang him a song with her beautiful voice.

My phone vibrated so I pulled it out. I read a text that said, *We got the boy.* I didn't even respond. I just put my phone back in my pocket and watched as my son let his mama's voice rock him to sleep. I suppose I had started noddin again because out of nowhere pandemonium hit the third floor like a bomb blast. I heard, "Code blue, room 3017, code blue, room 3017. I repeat, code blue, room 3017." I sat there getting my mind together then thought, *we in Jonathan's room, which is 3015, well damn, that's Jude's room they talking about.* As soon as that thought was complete I heard all kinds of feet running in the direction of my youngest son's room. I hopped up outta my chair so fast that it hit the floor with a loud thud. The bells and whistles on Jonathan's monitors started going off, and when I looked down at my son, I saw a graveyard full of sadness. That shit was palpable too, because I felt that misery myself, and couldn't say shit when I saw his fresh tears. I turned away and headed for the door. I heard Sophia call my name but ignored her crippled ass as I went to see what the hell was going on.

When I walked out of Jonathan's room and looked to my left, I saw all kinds of white coats standing around Jude's door. His bodyguard was standing off to the side so I walked towards that nigga to find out what the hell was going on. When he saw me coming, he started looking around, trying to evade my gaze. When we were standing chest to chin, I didn't say shit, just put my hands in my pockets and gave his ass a stare down that said, *Talk, muthafucka!* His damn eyes were big as hell and he had huge drops of sweat running down his face. I listened intently as my man started stuttering, talking about Jude's heart had stopped. I zoned him out and looked over my shoulder. Because I was a head taller than all the doctors standing in Jude's door I could see directly into his room and saw somebody beating on his chest while people were running around doing what the head honcho told them to do. But the crazy thing is, although those people were all over the place, trying to save my son's life, it was like they steered clear of his face because I could see that mug as clear as day from where I stood. His head looked as if it had gotten bigger since my initial visit, damn near twice its original size. I shifted my eyes to his body and noticed that when those people pushed on his chest his arms flopped around like a damn rag doll's. My ass knew death when I saw it and I knew my muthafuckin' son was gone. I put my eyes on Jude's closed lids and all I saw was dead man's eyes. *Soooo did those punk ass bitches just kill my son? Did those punk ass niggas just blow out my boy's candle?*

My mind went blank as my temple started pulsating. I could feel my pulse pounding in my neck and on my wrist. I could hear my heart beating in my ears, *"whoosh whoosh...whoosh whoosh."* That rhythm was so loud it took me back to when Sophia was pregnant with Jacob.

"Whoosh whoosh...whoosh whoosh." I'd gone to one of her doctor's appointments because she was having one of those suck up all ya money ultrasound visits, and the same shit I'd heard on that monitor was the same shit I heard in my ears. I watched them work on Jude for a good 30 minutes. I finally said, "Tell them bitches to get up off my son." *Whoosh whoosh...whoosh whoosh.* I guess nobody heard me because nobody moved, or maybe I whispered the shit and didn't know it. If that was the case, I made sure they heard me the second time. I looked over to my son's bodyguard, and his ass musta known Jude was gone too because he'd put some space between us and was staring dead at me. *"Whoosh whoosh...whoosh whoosh.* I put up my forefinger and beckoned him in my direction. When he reached my side I said, "Looka here, I know these muthafuckas' names cause the shits on they lab coats. Let them know that the next hands that are going to be touching my son's body is mine and his mama's and that if they don't get the fuck outta my son's room, Dr. Luke, Nurse Eve, Nurse Tabitha, Dr. Tirzah, Dr. Huldah." *Whoosh whoosh...whoosh whoosh.* My man tried to stop me

from naming names, like he got the point but was getting frustrated at the same time because I wouldn't shut up.

Whoosh whoosh...whoosh whoosh. I grabbed that little midget by his shirt collar, threw him up against the wall and said, "Nigga! You better go tell those peckerwoods, chinks, and Arabs to get the fuck outta my son's room. Like I said, Nurse Eve, Dr. Orpha, Dr. Luke and muthafuckin' Nurse Shilo Nigga you hear me, nigga? Huh? Or I swear to God yo dick gon be shoved down yo fuckin' throat tonight, bitch!" **Whoosh whoosh...whoosh whoosh.**" Sophia had been wheeled down to Jude's room, something I hadn't taken notice of until I heard, "Joseph?" I looked down at the mother of my baby boy and my look told her everything I couldn't. She said my name again but I didn't answer, all I could do was look at her pretty face turn into a horrific frown, then I looked between her legs and watched a puddle form as she pissed on herself.

My man didn't have to tell those doctors shit because when I let homeboy down and turned around they were all looking at me. They had looks on their faces like somebody in their group had a straightjacket and they were waiting on the perfect opportunity to catch me slipping so that they could pounce on my ass and put it on. I guess they had called the code too because when I looked over everybody's heads I saw Jude's still body lying in the bed with no one around it. I put my eyes back on Sophia and was surprised that she hadn't burst into tears. I heard somebody say, "Time of death?"

Then the answer, "3:25 p.m." Everybody started dispersing with their heads down in sadness, trying to avoid eye contact. I heard the staff mumbling, "Sorry for your loss" as they slowly moved to computers to write down the day's events. Somebody was closing Jude's door but I put my foot in that bitch then kicked it open. As I walked in I heard somebody stammer, "Mr. Amos, we want to make your son's body presentable and clean up his room before we let people in." I kept right on walking. They had me fucked up if they thought I was going to walk away from this tragedy and come back at a later time. I made my way to his bed as people worked around me, turning off monitors, picking up syringes and throwing away trash. I looked down at Jude and noticed he still had the tube in his mouth that had provided him life. I turned around and told anybody who would listen that the tube needed to be removed. About five minutes later a respiratory therapist came in and handled my request. As the tube was being taken out I heard what sounded like a pocket of air being expelled after it. That fucked me up because I sure in the hell thought it was his last breath although I hadn't seen his chest move for a few minutes. I watched as the staff changed his sheets, cleaned up his body and made it as to where it looked like my boy was in a peaceful sleep. I pulled up a chair and sat down. I heard people come and go as Sophia's church family offered her support. I didn't look up or acknowledge any of them; I just kept my eyes on my boy. From the time my family got to the hospital till that very moment, the hypocrites had been lurking in every corner. Even when Sophia and Shalom were admitted, they held vigil. I don't know if they asses thought they were incognito or what, hell, as far as I know maybe they didn't give a damn, but every time I came into a room, they walked out and every time I left a room, they walked in. I didn't sweat it though, because I knew Sophia needed the support, and it wasn't no big deal now because once I hit the streets, there was no guarantee I was coming back alive.

~SOPHIA~

Why do I feel like I'm being flipped like a pancake? And why do I keep hearing 3:25 p.m. in my head? Whose beautiful voices am I hearing? The sound is so pretty. I'm sleepy.

~JOSEPH~

After Shalom was born, I knew there weren't no more kids coming up in my crib, so I made Sophia get her damn tubes tied, otherwise she'd have kept right on havin' them. I know she thought I wasn't hip to her game by getting pregnant every other damn year, but I was, I ain't stupid. And she wasn't the first of my hoes to get pregnant either, but I made them other bitches get abortions cause I wasn't trying to have no ugly ass kids walking around with my name tattooed on they chest. So with Jude being the last of the Mohicans, I knew my lineage stopped with him. And although I wasn't really what you could call "close" to any of my kids, Jude was the child I really steered clear of because every time I looked down at his little ass, all I saw was the face of The Bitch.

As soon as I laid eyes on him, from day one, I saw Joanna. It was like he knew I wasn't feeling that shit because his little eyes, even at a few minutes old, followed me around the room wherever I walked. That shit was creepy as hell too.

It was almost like that little nigga could see into my soul or sumthin'. When Sophia brought him home, same shit, watching every move I made. Even when me and Sophia was fuckin', I'd look over at his little bassinet and his eyes would be dead on me. I shut that shit down real quick and told Sophia his little bitch ass had to vacate my throne because he was doin' the most. Hell, wasn't nobody running shit up in my piece but me. I don't know what it was about baby boy but he sensed I didn't want to be bothered, and as little dude grew up, he pushed that sensitive shit to the side, ignored how I felt, and began to stick to me like glue.

After Sophia had Shalom it seemed as if her sickly ass was always somewhere laid up with an ailment. On more than a few occasions I had to have a hoe or two shoot through to help her out around the house and since I was always about my paper, the coins I lost came outta her weekly allowance. During one such ailment Jacob and Jonathan both had back to back peewee football tournaments and as luck would have it Sophia's ass was out for the count. All three of my boys were super hyper and always pushing Sophia to the limit so she kept the two oldest active in any and everything she could find to keep them occupied. Chess, sports, karate, even dance lessons and it wasn't no faggot shit either, she knew how I got down. Naturally, Jude wanted to do everything he saw his big brothers doing, which pissed me the hell off. It didn't matter if they were outside playing kickball with the neighborhood kids or if I was shooting words of wisdom with Jacob and Jonathan. Jude would force his way into the huddle, and although I would kick him to the curb, his little butt would take a thousand ass whoopins just to be in our presence.

Any stupid ass knew my sons needed a ride along with the presence of an adult for whatever activity they were in, and this time wasn't no different. In the past, If Sophia was down, I would send one of my workers to fill in, but for some reason Jonathan and Jacob wanted so bad for me to take 'em. They begged me daily and got on my damn nerves while doing so, until I threatened to beat they asses. I was all for my kids doing extra shit, especially since I missed out as a kid, but that was Sophia's thang, not mine. And besides all that, I had been dealing with a whole lotta extra out in them streets, and was contemplating laying low for a few days. It seemed as if my putting my foot in somebody's ass was slowly catching up with me, and trouble was brewing around the corner.

When dealing with my property, I did things the same way a Fortune 500 company did business, but instead of surprising my employees with a random drug test, I did random body checks, spreading ass cheeks and all. Two weeks prior to the boys' tournament I had noticed that three of my hoes had been making their deposits with bruises on their body, and as luck would have it, it turned out to be one john who had been knocking my girls around. All three of the hoes said that they didn't want to rat the cat out because of the cheese he spread before them. I called them bitches in one at a time, politely beat they asses, and let them know that them decisions ain't theirs to make. They were also scared to tell me who the cat was, like they knew some shit I didn't, but my switchblade being placed on the table loosened those tongues. *How the hell you gon work for me but fear another nigga in the streets? Fuck that!* I beat they asses for that shit too. When they vomited out his name, I was like, *Damn, that nigga is a hefty payer, but naw, he gots to be dealt wit,* and commenced to personally reach out and touch that ass, then politely let him know that his means of apology could be made in any denomination. That muthafucka had to be crazy to have thought he could mess up my coins and get away with it. Hell, the clientele I dealt with didn't want no bruised up bitches, them rich muthafuckas wanted damn near perfection, so that's what the hell I gave 'em, and they paid well for it.

The streets were talking and the shit they were saying caused a nigga to rethink some moves. I learned that the john I had fucked up's uncle was no other than Mr. Samuel Dorcas, the crooked ass chief of police, who himself had used my services more times than I could count. Word had it that homeboy was using his weight to kick in every door in the hood trying to find out who'd put they foot in his nephew's ass, which prompted me to stay out the streets and under the radar. When those paved roads got to the temperature of an inferno, I shut my little men up by asking them what positions they played in football, because Daddy had flipped the script and was takin' 'em. I wasn't tryin to do no time over a dime so the day before Jonathan and Jacob's tournament, I had a change of heart and taking my sons to their game couldn't have come at a better time.

The boys were super hyped, but especially Jude. You'd have thought his ass was on a team the way he was actin. I took my boys to their game and I must say, they made me proud as hell. I sat in those stands shocked as I watched my sons topple and tumble over their miniature nemesis. I had never taken them to any of their extracurricular activities, so this was all new to me. Shit, Jonathan had to tell me how to get to the field and where to park. I sat back in awe of all the hype. The support these kids were getting carried big weight with their parents and siblings. Everybody was dressed in their team colors, screaming at the top of their lungs, hoping their voices would travel through the stadium, penetrate their sibling's or child's ear, and prompt a touchdown. Of course, Jude's worrisome ass was right there yelling and screaming his big brothers on. Every now and then I would take my eyes off the field, look down at him, and look into his eyes. That shit was weird as hell because it would be like I was looking into the eyes of The Bitch, except every time I looked into Jude's, I saw softness and innocence. Growing up The Bitch had eyes that were so hard it was like staring at cement, but not so with Jude. For a split second I wondered if The Bitch had ever had eyes like that. I dropped that thought like hot grits poppin' into my own damn eye, shifted my focus back to the field, and continued to watch my sons.

Towards the end of the game, Jude told me he had to pee. I looked down at him and thought, *I knew I shoulda left yo little ass at home.* Going to the bathroom wasn't rocket science, but it was for me. The only troubleshooting I had ever done in my life was making sure I didn't have trouble shooting a nigga in they ass, so I was not trying to find a bathroom in a damn unfamiliar stadium filled to the brink with people. I started to tell his butt to hold it until after the game and that he had bet not piss his pants but then he started doing a two-step dance. *Damn!* I started looking around for a sign that said bathroom, and as I did I had this strange feeling that I was being watched which caused me to feel real uncomfortable. It wasn't like a street alert, it was something different and I couldn't put my finger on it. I threw that thought over my shoulder and started walking towards the exit with Jude holding on to my leg for dear life. I asked one of the ushers where the bathroom was and if it had been a snake it woulda bit me because it was directly to my left. I drug Jude in there and stood watching as he went about taking care of his business but the first thing I noticed was that he went straight into the stall instead of going to the urinal. In my mind I thought, *well I'll be damned, his little ass don't even know how to piss. I'ma have a talk with Sophia bout this shit.* I opened the bathroom door, led him to the urinal, and then showed him how big boys use the bathroom. That little bit of attention from me brought such a big smile on his face I kinda started feeling bad for treating him the way I did, until his little dick ass pissed on my shoe. I jumped back which caused him to piss on his clothes and then on my shoes again. *Dammit!* My sudden movement scared the shit outta him so he had turned towards me in fear still pissing. I looked down at Jude with frustration written all over my face, and right before he was about to burst out into tears I closed my eyes and put my finger up to my lips. I wasn't for no whining ass kids, and although I know he wanted to bust a few tears, he didn't, cause he knew I would bust a few strokes on that ass. I pulled out my phone and called one of my workers and told him to get up there pronto. I then bent down to help Jude with his pants and gave him a little pep talk, letting him know that from now on, he needed to do like his big brothers and piss standing up. He shook his head up and down, elated that I was simply touching him.

I guess the game was close to being over because as we were walking out of the bathroom we were bum rushed by a crowd of men and boys coming in. I reached down and took the little man's hand while walking towards the exit. Game over for us cause I wasn't about to walk around with some pissy shoes on and a pissy kid trying to find Jonathan and Jacob. My phone rang and as I answered I saw the crowd thicken. It was my worker telling me that he was there. I told him to meet the boys at their locker room because I was out. He knew the location, it was my first time at the rodeo not his. I hung up and noticed Jude staring a whole through somebody, but by the time I had looked up, the person was ghost, or so I thought. Jude had a big smile on his face, and just as he was about to say something I felt somebody softly touch my hand and then I smelled her, Joanna.

I turned around so fast I tripped Jude and drug him on the floor. I did a quick sweep of the crowd with my eyes. *Damn!* The area was packed with people going in all kinds of directions so there wasn't no damn way I was going to find her ass, in spite of the fact that I was a head taller than everybody up in there. I knew that was The Bitch, I just knew it was. I looked down at Jude still on the floor looking like a little ragdoll as he held on to my hand like his little life depended on it. I yanked his ass up then headed for the exit door.

From that day forward, Jude became my right hand man. His ass had recognized The Bitch and I needed to know how. After leaving the stadium it took me thirty damn minutes to find my car, which added fuel to the flame. I was tempted to call my worker and have him, Jonathan and Jacob look for that bitch, but I wasn't for the extra noise I'd get from Jonathan and Jacob begging to ride home with me. Once I found my ride, I sat Jude's little pissy ass on a trash bag that

I got from out of my trunk and listened as he went on and on about his grandma as I drove us home. I was fuming! The more he talked, the madder I got. He said that he sees The Bitch all the time and that she pushes him on the swing whenever they go to the park. I listened to every single adjective that came outta little man's mouth and placed them all into my rolodex of time, making sure I didn't miss a damn syllable. I knew that in the near future I was going to hafta recall everything Jude was saying, so with that in mind, I kept every single word he spit out, along with the way he said it, in alphabetical fucking order.

When we got home I sent Jude to his room then went to check on Sophia. Her ass was in the bed looking all weak and shit so I quietly closed the door. I went into the boys' bathroom and started a bath for Jude. Although I was itching to get out of my pissy shit, I took care of him first. One of my hoes was taking care of Shalom and would have jumped if I'd told her to take pounce Jude, but after that bathroom incident with him sitting on the damn toilet, I thought, *Fuck it,* and took care of him myself. I was learning that bitches cain't teach kids every damn thang, boys anyway, so I didn't sweat it. As I watched Jude splash and play in the tub, my mind kept going back to things he had said. I could not believe Sophia had the balls to betray me like that. Did she really have the audacity to give The Bitch the privilege of seeing and touching my seed. Her ass was about to regret the day she ever made that asinine decision.

After I got Jude settled and in bed, I pulled up a little chair and had a bonding session with my baby boy. I told him that he was tell me every time he saw The Bitch and that it was our little secret, and that he wasn't to tell nobody. The vein in my forehead started throbbing when I heard that little nigga say, "That's what Grand mommy told me too, so ok," and then he whispered, "Our little secret, Daddy." I sat there for a long time, looking at absolutely nothing, trying not to lose my damn mind. After about an hour I pulled the blanket up to Jude's shoulders, rubbed him on the top of his sleeping head and then went looking for the hoe that was taking care of Shalom because I was about to fuck that bitch's back out.

Sophia knew something wasn't right. Six months after her recovery she jumped right back into Mommy mode but felt something in me had shifted. She steered clear and kept the kids out of my way too. At times I'd catch her looking at me out the corner of her eyes, but I'd act as if I hadn't noticed. I don't know if she was aware of the fact that every time Jude came home from an activity with The Bitch, he would sneak his little sneaky ass into whatever room I was in and give me the rundown. Naturally he'd find me flicking through channels, with the volume on mute, looking for that nigga, but everything would be put on pause whenever he came in. I'd unmute that shit and turn to cartoons. He had diarrhea of the mouth and withheld no details. The last straw came when Jude ran up to me and whispered, "Come here, Daddy," prompting me to come down to his level with his little finger.

I bent to my knees and said, "Wassup, lil man?"

Jude leaned in, kissed me on my lips and said, "I saw Grand mommy at the park today and she wanted me to give you a kiss from her. She kissed me on my lips and told me not to lick 'em or eat nothin' or drink nothin' until I gave you your kiss." Jude took his little hands, put them on my cheeks, and then started kissing me over and over again. I froze, heard a real loud ringing in my ears and then slapped Jude so hard his little ass was knocked into the other room. I shot up and floated up my spiral staircase like a spirit. Sophia had heard Jude wailing and ran out of the bedroom, but when she saw me floating in her direction she did a 360 and tried to shut and lock the bedroom door before I got there. I kicked that bitch open so hard the force knocked Sophia to the floor. She flipped onto her back trying to scoot away with a terrified look on her face. In the background I heard Jonathan shooing the boys to Shalom's room and lock the door. I grabbed Sophia by her leg and yanked her towards me. She was kicking and screaming as I punched her wherever my fist landed. Her dumb ass had the nerve to try to fight back. I grabbed her ass by her hair, and like Fred Flintstone, pulled her into the bathroom. I flipped up the toilet seat, grabbed her head with both my hands and pushed it into the toilet water. Her hands were digging into my wrist as I yelled, "You no good for nothing trick bitch you fucking bitch! You nasty ass hoe! You ready to die, bitch? Huh? You ready to die? You two cent whore!" Sophia was trying to use anything she could to get some leverage. Her legs were scraping against the floor as she fought to find her footing, trying her hardest to get up, but the toilet water prohibited that and made her slip and slide like wax paper. She had drawn blood while trying to loosen my grip from around her neck and had actually reached behind her back and scratched the fuck outta my face. How she managed to do that I'll never know, but I suppose when you dying you do shit you wouldn't ordinarily be able to do. My ass was foaming at the mouth as I squeezed the life out of Sophia.

She was starting to lose the fight as I tried to break her fucking neck in two. Her legs started slowing down and her grip on my hand was getting weaker. I pushed her head further down into the toilet and noticed some blood float up. I guess I'd busted her damn nose on that porcelain bowl because that last push made a big blood bubble float to the surface. Then out of nowhere I heard, "Joseph!"

I looked to my left and look straight into the eyes of The Bitch as Jude's little five year old ass said, "Get off my mama," pulled the trigger of my .38, flew back onto the floor because of the force, and shot me in my damn chest.

I was in the hospital for a whole six weeks and felt like it was overkill. When they came at me about some physical therapy I told they asses I was gone get physical if they didn't get me up out that bitch. I had some serious shit to take care of on the home front and there was nothing they could say to persuade me to stay another day. They reluctantly gave me my discharge papers but made sure they covered they asses by having me sign out AMA and by giving my doctor all the information he needed to continue my care at home. When it was about time for me to leave, my nurse brought a wheelchair into my room like I was really gon get in that shit. I looked at her like she had leprosy and then asked, "Who the fuck that for?" I was a grown ass man and was not about to be wheeled out no damn hospital like I was a cripple. With all the balloons, cards, bears and shit my hoes had sent me packed up, I threw my covers back and was about to stand up when I saw my nurse making a beeline to my bed with her arms stretched out yelling, "Nooo, I have to give you your blood pressure medicine!" Too late, as soon as my feet hit the floor and my knees started carrying my weight, them bitches buckled. All I saw was my face going towards my bedside table, then blackness.

When I opened my eyes two days later, the sunlight caused my head to hurt so bad I closed them mugs right back shut. I woke up a few hours later and my room was black as night, but my head wasn't hurting so I was good. As I was lifting my hand to my head to feel the damage I had done, I felt a hand on top of mine. When I looked down I saw Sophia with her head on my bed asleep. She still looked like the innocent child I'd picked up from the bus station a few years back and I'll be damned if her ass wasn't getting more beautiful every day.

While laid up, my workers kept me abreast of my business affairs on a day to day basis, but the only thing I was interested in hearing about was Sophia and the kids. It was the day before my "head first" tumble that they told me that her ass had packed up half my shit, the kids and bounced. I damn near hit the roof! Immediately my damn temple started pounding, which caused my fucking blood pressure to shoot sky high. All them damn bells and whistles started going off on my monitor and scared the shit outta me. But the momentum got even higher when my nurse ran her ass into my room with a syringe in her hand talkin' bout, "Mr. Amos, you need to stop getting yourself all worked up. You keep going at this pace you gon end up giving yourself a heart attack!" Her ass had the nerve to say that shit with a 'tude. I looked at her with venom in my eyes then opened my mouth to check her bold ass but couldn't because without warning, I broke out into a cold sweat and became short of breath. That shit happened so fast I didn't know what had hit me. My nurse put some oxygen in my nose while still running her trap, then started pushing my heart medication. I didn't give a rat's ass about nothin but catchin' my fuckin' breath. *Did that bitch just say heart attack? What the hell she talkin' bout? I ain't heart attack material.* Hell, I wasn't even 40 so what she said was straight foolishness, in my book anyway. As I began to settle down, I realized that not one time had Sophia brought her ass up to the hospital to see how I was doing after Jude's ass shot me, but the kicker was, she hadn't sent any of the kids up there either.

I had to reel in my shit or die. Basically that's what my cardiologist told me. I was no beat around the bush kinda nigga so I told my doctors to show me the same respect, but damn! I laid in that hospital bed scared to belch thinkin' I was gon roll over and die if I did. I ain't ashamed to say a nigga ain't for no needles or pain although I'll slit a trick's throat in two point two seconds with no hesitation, but this shit was foul. Once I got the ok to start living again I wanted to move with full speed ahead but was warned on more than one occasion to watch my diet and to stay out of stressful situations. I looked at them white coats like, *Whatever!* I'm a damn pimp, what the hell they mean stay outta stressful situations? I had more stress trying to manage a corner than the president had trying to run the whole damn country.

After the doctor had all my meds tapered and balanced, and instructions given to my personal physician, I was ready to get home to my own bed, especially since they'd unwillingly given me the all clear. That's when I'd fallen face first and ended up spending another two weeks in the damn hospital. Because of my newly diagnosed heart condition and head injury, my stay was made longer than I had anticipated. I guess my acting like a bitch after hearing about her packing up my shit, and kids, along with damn my near death experience in the process of trying to get up out that bitch, had reached her ears, because there she was, looking all innocent and shit. As I looked at her I realized that I hadn't come up with a solution to the whole getting shot by my five year old son situation yet. On the real, the damn temper tantrum I threw had nothing to do with the fact that Sophia took my shit and the kids. Hell naw, it was the fact that don't shit walk away from me unless I let it.

~

I was yanked outta memory lane when I heard a whole lotta damn screaming and hollering coming from outside my dead son's room. His door was damn near kicked opened as my bodyguards tried to contain a woman who looked like she was about to bust, and although it was illogical, her ass looked 12 damn months pregnant. I stood up and watched as she stopped, then stood completely still with her eyes glued to Jude. *Well I'll be damned!* I guess her ass was about to bust because as she stood there frozen, she slowly closed her eyes, screamed like she was being murdered, grabbed her stomach and then bent over just as her water broke. *Could this night get any fucking crazier? Well ain't this about a bitch!* I guess it could because right after that bitch's water broke, Jude's wife walked in.

~SOPHIA~

Proverbs 3:5
    5 Trust in the Lord with all your heart
        and lean not on your own understanding; 6 in
    all your ways submit to him,

and he will make your paths straight.

Oh yes, my favorite Bible verse!

Philippians 4:6

6 Be anxious for nothing, but in everything by prayer and supplication, with thanksgiving, let your requests be made known to God; 7 and the peace of God, which surpasses all understanding, will guard your hearts and minds through Christ Jesus.

Why do I keep hearing 3:25 p.m.?

Matthew 11:28

28 Come to me, all you who are weary and burdened, and I will give you rest. 29 Take my yoke upon you and learn from me, for I am gentle and humble in heart, and you will find rest for your souls. 30 For my yoke is easy and my burden is light.

What's that wet stuff on my face? Am I crying?

Mark 12:30

30 Love the Lord your God with all your heart and with all your soul and with all your mind and with all your strength'[a] 31 The second is this: 'Love your neighbor as yourself.'[b] There is no commandment greater than these."

Who's reading my favorite Bible verses to me?

John 10:10

10 The thief comes only to steal and kill and destroy; I have come that they may have life, and have it to the full.

I sure am hungry. I don't think I've eaten since yesterday.

John 16:33

33 I have told you these things, so that in me you may have peace. In this world you will have trouble. But take heart! I have overcome the world.

Yessss, another one of my favorites. Oh, that's sister Abel, what's she doing at my house? I wish I could wake up so I can tell her to leave before Joseph gets home.

Psalm 116

1 I love the Lord, for he heard my
   voice; he heard my cry for mercy.

2 Because he turned his ear to me, I
   will call on him as long as I live.

3 The cords of death entangled me,
   the anguish of the grave came over me; I
   was overcome by distress and sorrow.

4 Then I called on the name of the
   Lord: "Lord, save me!"

5 The Lord is gracious and righteous;
   our God is full of compassion.

6 The Lord protects the unwary;
   when I was brought low, he saved me. 7
Return to your rest, my soul,
   for the Lord has been good to you.

8 For you, Lord, have delivered me from
   death, my eyes from tears,
   my feet from stumbling, 9
that I may walk before the
Lord in the land of the living. 10 I
trusted in the Lord when I said, "I
     am greatly afflicted";

11 in my alarm I said,
   "Everyone is a liar."

12 What shall I return to the Lord
   for all his goodness to me?

13 I will lift up the cup of salvation

and call on the name of the Lord. 14
I will fulfill my vows to the Lord in
the presence of all his people. 15
Precious in the sight of the Lord
   is the death of his faithful servants. 16
Truly I am your servant, Lord;
   I serve you just as my mother did; you
   have freed me from my chains.
17 I will sacrifice a thank offering to you
   and call on the name of the Lord.
18 I will fulfill my vows to the Lord
   in the presence of all his people,
19 in the courts of the house of the
   Lord— in your midst, Jerusalem.
Praise the Lord.

I absolutely love reading and hearing God's word!
Mark 4:39

39 And he arose, and rebuked the wind, and said unto the sea, Peace, be still. And the wind ceased, and there was a great calm.

Why do I keep hearing 3:25 p.m.?

~JOSEPH~

I called my personal tailor so that he could come and take measurements of my son, and then outta nowhere I started hearing a tune in my head. Where that shit came from I don't know but it was a sweet drumbeat. Although unfamiliar, it sounded familiar at the same time. I sat back down in my chair and let them two bitches behind me do what bitches do. I started tapping my feet to the beat in my head.

Bruuummm, bruuummm, brum, brum BRUM! Bruuummm, bruuummm, brum brum BRUM! Then it got faster *bruuummmbruuummmbrumbrumBRUM.* I started tapping my hands on my legs as my symphony of nothingness played. *Bruuummm, bruuummm, brum, brum, BRUM.* That shit played for ten damn minutes and as it played, I got more and more into the rhythm. I thought, *under different circumstances this shit would be tight! Shiiiid, I would even grab Sophia and dance with her ass if she was next to me.* But she wasn't next to me, she was down the hall sedated and Jacob was on life support, and Shalom was doped up not able to cope with reality and Jonathan was tied down like a fucking animal trying not to flip outta his bed while having damn seizures and my goddamn baby boy was dead. Awww shit!, the beats gettin' better *bruuummm, bruuummm, brum, brum, BRUM.* I should go find Sophia. *Bruuummm, bruuummm, brum, brum, BRUM.* Damn, this shit is intense. *Bruuummm, bruuummm, brum, brum, BRUM. Bruuummm*

(I!) bruuummm (COULD!) brum (LISTEN!) brum (TO!) BRUM (THIS!) bruuummm (SHIT!) bruuummm (ALL!) brum (DAMN!) brum (DAY!) BRUM! BRUUUMMMBRUUUMMMBRUMBRUMBRUM!

I stopped moving to the beat because the music stopped playing. I thought, *why in the fuck did the music stop? Whelp, them niggas gon wish that damn song had played forever cause it's time for me to go peel some potatoes and split some muthafuckin' wigs.* I stood up, walked over to the little nigga that tried to kill me due to his love for his mama, and stared down at his shell. I put his puffy hand in mine then bent down and gave baby boy a kiss on his lips. Them bitches were still kinda warm. I put my cheek on his then whispered, "Tell The Bitch I said I'll see her soon" and then walked outta his room...to be continued...

~JOANNA~

I grew up in a middle class family with parents who worked hard to get a decent little brick house on a nice quiet street where neighbors quickly became best friends. Both my parents worked at the post office and back in those days that was the ideal job with government benefits that allowed us regular dental visits and good healthcare for broken arms. We were a family that took vacations every year and my mom has a closet filled with photo albums to prove it. I'm the youngest of three, the only girl and I'm spoiled rotten. I was my father's pride and joy along with my mother's adored real live baby doll. Although my brothers, Jonathan, the oldest and Jude the middle child, were a couple of years older than me, they were never jealous of the attention I received. Shoot, they showered me with just as much attention as my parents did and I rarely had to lift a finger when they were around. We were a blessed family by all accounts. My dad was the preacher of the congregation we attended, which is why people still ask the question, *"With everything her parents and brothers did for her, how in the hell did she end up the way she did?"* And as with most little sheltered girls who go astray, the answer is the same, a boy.

Although I was 13, and the child of God fearing parents, I've always had a side of me that wanted to burst free like a butterfly and spread my wings. I was hella sneaky, and although my parents weren't stupid, for the most part, they believed just about everything I told them, even if it was a lie.

109

But, if I got caught in the act of doing something I wasn't supposed too, I had hell to pay and they showed me no mercy.

I remember I had taken some money from Jonathan's piggy bank because I'd heard the ice-cream truck and didn't have money of my own. I was probably about seven at the time, which means I knew better. I took the money and didn't get just one, but two ice-cream sandwiches, and wouldn't give any to Jude or Jonathan. My brothers shared a room, and out of frustration, Jonathan stormed to the bedroom and slammed his door, which caused his piggy bank to fall off the dresser and burst open onto the floor. He immediately noticed that no bills had fallen out, just his change, and stormed to my parents' room with proof that I'd stolen money from him to get ice-cream. Now, I knew I was a daddy's girl, but I also knew that if Daddy's two eyebrows became one because of the frown on his face, I was in big trouble. After Jonathan snitched, my dad came storming out of his bedroom with that one eyebrow and my heart skipped a beat. We all knew one thing, and that was to not get on Daddy's bad side, and that included my mama. My daddy took three big steps towards me, picked me up by my little bony arms, knocked that ice-cream outta my hand and carried me to my bedroom. While bent over his shoulder I screamed, *"I'm sorry, Daddy, I'm sorry! I won't do it no more, I promise...Daddy please,"* as Jude and Jonathan looked at me with sorrow in their eyes. That day I got a beat down to remember and you had best believe I didn't steal another thing, that is, until Rufus. After my dad finished my whooping, he called Jonathan into my room and told him to go get a wet face towel, and when Jonathan returned, Daddy sat me on his lap and wiped my tears away. That cool wetness felt so good on my hot face that as he wiped I pushed my face deeper into its coolness. After I had stopped snotting and hiccupping and mumbling, my dad called both my brothers into my room and told all three of us why stealing was a sin and how God sees and views people who steal. By the time he'd finished my head was leaned against his shoulders and I promised to never steal again as his strong arms held me close. Later that night Jude came into my room and held me in his arms. He told me that all I had to do was ask and he would have given me the money and that what Daddy said was right, and that I knew better. As he talked I looked over his shoulder and saw my beautiful mom stick her head into my room. When I looked into her eyes they said, *"I love you"* as she gave me a faint smile and blew me a kiss. I blew her one back as she slowly closed the door so that my Jude could continue ministering to me.

Childhood memories are to be cherished and held on to. When we were younger our dad would sit us all at his feet and read the Bible to us every night before we went to bed. Some people may have thought that was cheesy, but not us. That was our norm and in our eyes, our hero was feeding us the bread of life and we never wanted a crumb to be wasted. Those are memories we all cherished and clung on to, especially when life got hard. During the hard times my siblings and I could always look back and envision our big gentle giant of a dad reading us, "What thus saith the Lord" and hold on to whatever truth that came into our head. Or, how when Mama would be cooking Sunday dinner on Saturday night she'd always let us help, and it would be during those moments that she would talk to us about the kind of mate we should desire, so that we could have good peaceable lives. She would always throw little hints out there too, like sister Miriam's daughter, Abagail. Mama would go on and on about how pretty she was, and how chaste and quiet she was, and how she and Jude would make a beautiful God fearing couple. Or how brother Crispus nephew, Timothy, who visited every year, was going to the school of preaching once he graduated high school because he wanted to be about the Lord's business and become a teacher of the gospel. When I was young, I used to cherish those talks, but as I got older, I couldn't wait for her to shut up because the more she talked, the longer it would be before I would be able to sneak out to see Rufus.

About Angela Moore

Angela Moore has worked as a respiratory therapist at the VA Hospital in Indianapolis for fourteen years. The biological mother of three (but mother to many) is a faithful member of her church and the grandmother of two. In her spare time, she enjoys roller-skating, swimming, and fellowshipping with friends and family, both near and far.

www.ingramcontent.com/pod-product-compliance
Lightning Source LLC
Chambersburg PA
CBHW060829250626
47162CB00005B/2004